The
Missing Ballerina Mystery

School for Stars

The

Missing Ballerina Mystery

Holly & Kelly Willoughby

Orion
Children's Books

First published in Great Britain in 2015
by Orion Children's Books
an imprint of Hachette Children's Group
and published by Hodder and Stoughton Limited
Carmelite House
50 Victoria Embankment
London EC4Y 0DZ
An Hachette UK Company

1 3 5 7 9 10 8 6 4 2

A catalogue record for this book is available from the British Library

ISBN 978 1 4440 1457 0

www.orionchildrensbooks.com

To l'Etoilettes everywhere who are seeking answers.
Sometimes all you have to do is slow down,
take a step back and you might just find that
what you're looking for is right under your nose.

Contents

Welcome back, Story-seeker, to a new and exciting adventure with our favourite girls.

After an uncharacteristically quiet term at their beloved L'Etoile, our girls have arrived in London for the summer holidays and are itching for adventure!

Maria is ready to shadow journalist Luscious Tangerella at the Gazette, while Molly and the rest of the gang are determined to seek out some mischief. Who knows what they'll find, but if you know our L'Etoilettes as well as we do, Story-seeker, they'll be slipping into their black assassin gear for a midnight escapade in no time!

So sit comfortably and float into the Mystery of the Missing Ballerina.

Enjoy!

Love
Holly and Kelly Willoughby x

1

Double Trouble in London

'Maria! What are you scrambling about under that desk for this time?' Molly asked her sister.

'My lucky silver pen . . . it's missing. There's no way I can go to the *Gazette* without it . . . I alllllllways have it!' Maria said in despair.

Molly looked fondly at her usually calm and collected twin. To say she was finding the sight of Maria flapping about like a headless chicken amusing was an understatement. The Easter holidays had been a complete disaster for Maria, after her journalist hero, Luscious Tangerella, or LT as she was now referred to, had cancelled Maria's promised week of shadowing her at the *Gazette* due to Buckingham

Palace announcing the birth of a royal baby. LT had had to drop everything in order to put together a special issue, which had left Maria twiddling her thumbs at home.

And we all know that boredom and disappointment, for someone as intelligent as Maria, Story-seeker, might possibly be the worst combination!

'Right, when did you last have this super-duper pen?' Molly asked, deciding it would be better for everyone if the elusive pen was found or none of them would be allowed to go to sleep that night.

'I was sitting on my bed writing today's *to do* list, then I put my notebook down . . .' Maria said thoughtfully.

'Where . . . where did you put it down? I can't see your notebook either,' Molly said, looking in Maria's bedside cabinet and under the bed.

'I know! How can I have been so forgetful? I put it where I always put it, in case I suddenly wake up in the night and think of something important . . . *et voila*!' Maria announced in her best French accent as she flung her pillow on the floor.

'You sleep with a notebook and pen under your

pillow?' Molly said in disbelief. She'd heard everything now.

'Of course. Nothing more frustrating than having a brilliant idea in your dreams, then waking up and not being able to remember what it was. I bet you sleep with something completely ridiculous under your pillow!' said Maria, leaping over to Molly's bed.

Molly dived after her. 'Nooooooo!' she cried, but it was too late. There, in a little sparkly photo frame, was a picture of Prince Henry, heir to the throne, and in Molly's mind, her future husband. 'I can't believe you just did that!' Molly yelped like a wounded puppy. 'I only discovered what you hide under your pillow because I was trying to be helpful. Are we not allowed to have any secrets?'

'Not when you're a twin, Moll!' Maria giggled.

'YO!' came a shout from the hall. 'What's all the racket about?' asked Sally as she entered the room.

'You don't want to know!' Molly and Maria said in unison, then burst out laughing, thinking how equally silly they had been.

'Good!' Sally said. 'Well, if you've quite finished with your morning row, we should go outside and wait for Pippa. She'll be here any minute!'

'Woohoo!' Molly said. 'I can't believe we've been

off school a whole week already and away from our darling Pippa.'

'Just think how sad you'd both be if you didn't have me living with you either,' Sally said confidently.

Sally's mum, Maggie Sudbury, had come to work for the Fitzfoster family a year ago, and it was the perfect arrangement for the three girls. It meant that they were always together, during term time and in the holidays. Even if they were in the London house and Maggie had to stay on in the country at Wilton House, the twins made sure Sally never left their side.

'Exactly Sal! You're like our AT,' Molly said, grabbing her hand.

'AT?' Even Maria had no idea what AT meant.

'Adopted triplet . . . obvs!' Molly grinned.

'Ha . . . only without the arguments!' said Sally. 'Which I'm more than happy about, BTW!'

 (BTW = By the way, Story-seeker)

'It's such a flipping shame the Sawyers aren't in London for the hols. It's so typical. When we were in the countryside for Christmas, Danya and Honey were in London and now that we're in London, they're in the country! Honestly, you couldn't make it up!' Molly groaned.

'It's not their fault they had to go to their grandparents in Norfolk. I bet they'd rather be here with us too,' Maria said.

And they would have, Story-seeker, or at least in a house ten seconds' walk away. Since Molly and Maria had met the Sawyer twins at the start of last term, the coincidences had just kept on coming . . . even down to where their parents lived. As fate would have it, the Sawyers lived on the other side of Beaufort Square, at number forty-four. This was discovered, to the girls' delight, when Mrs Fitzfoster had asked for their home address to invite them to the Fitzfoster party in the caves under Wilton House. In the words of our Molly, Story-seeker – WATC?

 (WATC = What are the chances?)

It had only been a week since L'Etoile broke up but it already felt like a lifetime. Pippa's cousin had got married that weekend in Cornwall, so she'd gone straight from L'Etoile to the venue to help her family with all the wedding preparations and rehearse for her performance in the church. But now she was on the way to join her best friends for some London mischief!

Beaufort Square was one of those beautiful London squares with terraced town houses on three sides, a church at one end and an immaculate, private garden in the middle. It never looked more breath-taking than in the summer, when everything was green and leafy.

'I think this might be my very favourite time of the year,' Molly said, basking in the warm sunshine.

'You said that at Christmas!' Maria groaned.

'Can I help it if I appreciate the beauty of Mother Nature?' Molly said.

'Sure, because the mountain of Christmas presents under our tree had nothing to do with why you said that was your favourite time of year!' Maria said.

'Are you two at it again?' Sally said. 'Honestly, what's got into you today?'

'Don't look at me,' Molly said. 'She's really tetchy today. I can't say or do anything without her jumping down my throat.'

'I'm sorry,' Maria said, immediately realising that

the girls were right. 'I think it's just my nerves for tomorrow. I've been looking forward to it for so long, now that it's finally here, it's all a bit much to compute. What if I mess up . . . trip up . . . or even throw up!'

'You'll be fine, Mimi,' Molly said, suddenly feeling guilty for snapping. Of course Maria was nervous. 'Honestly, Mimi, this is what you've been waiting for your whole life. You have nothing to worry about. You were born to be a journalist! Now tell me, what are you going to wear?'

'What am I going to wear?' Maria turned white. 'I haven't even thought about that!'

Molly raised every eyebrow she had . . . well, all two of them.

To Molly Fitzfoster, our resident fashion queen, Story-seeker, the world began and ended with glamour and sparkle, so the fact that Maria hadn't even planned what she might wear for the most important week of her life was unthinkable!

'You haven't thought about your outfit? You must be joking. You're kidding . . . right?' she said hesitantly.

'To be truthful, it totally slipped my mind. I've been thinking more about researching what's going on in

the world this week so I can contribute in meetings,'
Maria said.

'Well now, sister dear. Isn't it lucky that you have
Beaufort Square's top fashionista to help you dress to
impress?' Molly said with a dazzling smile.

Sally giggled. This was where Molly would get
her own back on her stressed out, snappy sister. She
could see it now. A whole afternoon of make-up and
curling tongs lay ahead, and that was before she'd
tried anything on.

Molly had her thinking cap on. A multitude of
looks flashing through her mind.

Suddenly she was distracted by a large silver car
sweeping past them only to screech to a halt a bit
further down the road.

'Pippa!' Sally squealed, running down the street.

As she did, the back doors flew open and who
should jump out but Danya and Honey Sawyer.
Molly, Maria and Sally couldn't believe their eyes.
Was it really them? But they were in Norfolk!

As they got closer, they saw that it was them. The
Sawyers were in London!

*Finally, someone sensible to talk through her week
with*, Maria thought, pleased to have Danya back.

Finally, someone to talk fashion with, Molly thought,

ecstatic at seeing Honey.

How brilliant, but I hope Pippa gets here soon. I miss my pretend twin, Sally thought.

'Girls! What on earth are you doing here?' Molly said, throwing her arms around Honey, then Danya.

'We thought you were in Norfolk for the holidays,' Maria exclaimed.

'We were!' Danya said. 'But the stupid builders working on Granny and Grandpa's house didn't shut the water supply off properly when they disconnected the kitchen pipes and the whole ground floor of the house flooded overnight. Honestly, it's such a mess up there. I feel so sorry for them.'

'Oh no – what a nightmare for them, but what a dream for us!' Sally said.

'Does this mean that you're staying here for the rest of the hols then?' Molly asked, hopefully.

'Yessssirrreee!' Honey squealed. 'Can you believe it? And we've only got Greta to keep an eye on us so we're in the clear for mischief. Mum and Dad have stayed on in Norfolk to help.'

'Greta?' Molly asked.

'Our au pair,' Danya said. 'She's over from Berlin for the holidays to help look after us. She's really sweet, but thankfully quite naive so we're not having too much trouble running rings around her.'

'Sounds perfect to me!' Maria said with a wink.

'What are you doing out here in the square anyway?' Danya asked. 'It's as if you were waiting for us!'

'Pippa's arriving any second now,' Sally said excitedly.

'No way! That's amazing. The whole gang's together. Or at least we will be. How about we go home, get unpacked and then pop over to yours later for a proper catch-up?' Honey suggested.

'Brilliant!' Molly said. 'Give us an hour to settle Pippa in and put in some Mum-and-Dad time. We live at number seven.'

'Coolio! See you later, *London Girls*!' Honey shouted back before jumping in the car next to an exasperated-looking Greta, who'd been trying to get the twins' attention since they'd decided to jump out so suddenly.

'How fab is this?' Molly said.

'I know. It couldn't have worked out any better if we'd planned it,' Maria said, having quite forgotten all about her *Gazette* nerves.

'Pippa!' all three girls shouted, seeing Uncle Harry's red car pull up alongside them.

'Pippa!' Sally cried as she opened the car door. 'Thank

goodness you're here. I was starting to feel like a right gooseberry with the twin explosion on this square!'

'What?' Pippa said, confused.

'Pippa, you won't believe it . . . the Sawyers are here too! They've just arrived,' Molly said. 'The whole gang's back together!'

'Wow, that's amazing news!' Pippa grinned and then turned to Sally. 'I'll be your honorary twin any day, Sal!'

Sally beamed.

'That was the longest car journey from Devon. I think it was made even worse because I've been dying to see you all,' Pippa said, dragging her case up the front steps.

'It's all right for you, Pippa,' Uncle Harry said, closing the boot. 'I've got to do the whole thing again tomorrow when I go and collect your mum. Why she couldn't get the train, I'll never know!'

'Ah I know, Uncle H. You're the best. Thanks so much for dropping me off. Drive safely and I'll phone you tomorrow,' Pippa said, kissing him goodbye.

Uncle Harry stood for a moment, just watching the gaggle of giddy girls all talking over each other. 'No problem, Pippy. Just mind your manners and don't go getting into any mischief,' he said.

'Yeah, right!' Pippa said, flashing him a smile.

And with that the London threesome, which had unexpectedly turned into a fivesome, became a complete, mischievous sixsome!

2

Catching Up

'Mrs Dundas! Look who's here!' Molly said as the four girls burst in through the front door.

Mrs Dundas was the Fitzfosters' housekeeper at number seven. She was the loveliest lady and, more importantly, the best cook ever.

Well, nearly the best cook ever, Story-seeker. Sally's mum, Maggie, still held the trophy for the tastiest chocolate brownies on the planet.

'Lovely to meet you, Pippa. The twins and Sally have told me so much about you. Are you hungry, dear?' Mrs Dundas asked as she took some of Pippa's bags.

'If your legendary flapjack is on offer, I'm hungry,' Pippa said, her mouth watering. 'You see, I've heard all about you too!'

Mrs Dundas blushed with pride. 'Coming right up, girls. I tell you what, why don't you take Pippa's things and show her where she's sleeping and I'll bring a tray of goodies up for you.'

'Perfect!' Maria said, grabbing everything back from Mrs Dundas.

'Follow me, Pippa,' Sally said. 'You're bunking in with me. Wait till you see our room. It's so cool. We've got our own bathroom and everything.'

'Mu-um!' Molly called up the stairs. 'Pippa's here.'

Linda Fitzfoster peered over the bannister. 'Hello, Pippa, darling. How wonderful to see you. The girls have missed you so much. How was the wedding?'

'Oh it was so beautiful, Mrs F. My cousin looked like a princess and the sun shone the whole day,' Pippa said.

'What did you sing?' Maria asked.

'I cheated a bit and sang the same song I wrote for Mrs Fuller's wedding – but none of the guests had heard it before so it was like singing it for the first time,' Pippa answered. 'Everyone seemed to like it.'

'I love that song! Your voice gives me more and

more goose-bumps every term since you've been at L'Etoile,' Molly said.

'Ah thanks, Moll,' Pippa said.

'Will you sing it for us, please?' Sally asked.

'Oh yes – that would be lovely, Pippa. I'm pleased to say Mr Fitzfoster will be home in time to join us for dinner so maybe you could do it then, by way of a little after-dinner entertainment?' Linda Fitzfoster said.

'Sure! I'd love to!' Pippa replied.

'Come on then – let's go upstairs – or our flapjacks will arrive before we do!' Molly said. 'See you later, Mum!'

Linda Fitzfoster smiled as she watched the four best friends disappear to their bedrooms. They really did love each other to pieces and it was a pleasure to see.

While Sally helped Pippa unpack, Molly dived straight into her extensive wall of wardrobes.

'Right, Maria . . . here's what I'm thinking . . .'

'Oh, I'd forgotten about this,' Maria said, suddenly reminded of her Gazette nerves, and remembering the outfit marathon ahead.

'How about this emerald top, with these skinnies and black pumps. I haven't worn any of them yet. In fact I ordered the top from *www.looklikeastar.com*

with you in mind anyway. This shade of green will bring out the colour of your eyes.'

As Molly laid everything out on the bed for Maria's approval, Maria could have kissed her. It was perfect. Simple, yet classy; chic yet saying 'I mean business'. And what's more, she hadn't even had to try fifty things on to find it.

'Spot on, Moll! You really have found your calling. Just think, a journalist and a stylist in one family. Together, we'll rule the world!' Maria said as she started to undress.

'I'd hope there might be an actress in there somewhere too, but right now I'll take what I can get!' Molly said, admiring her handiwork.

'That looks fab, Maria,' Sally said as she came in.

'How do you feel?' asked Pippa. 'Sally said you're a bit nervous.'

'I feel so much better now. I think I just needed you girls around me to take my mind off things,' Maria said, admiring herself in the mirror.

'Just think, this time tomorrow you might be phoning us with a new mystery to solve after hearing what they're all working on at the *Gazette*!' Pippa said.

'I know. I can't believe it's been so long. How boring was last term? Literally nothing but work,

work, work. I almost wished Lucifette had come back to L'Etoile to annoy us. At least we always a good-versus-evil mission on our hands while she was around,' Maria said.

'Oh don't say that. Never wish that monster back into our lives. I've wasted far too much of my life living in her spiteful shadow,' Sally said quickly.

I think it's fair to say, Story-seeker, that Sally Sudbury would be forever nervous at the mention of her old companion, Lucinda Marciano, who thankfully was expelled from L'Etoile at the end of last year. Still, she and her mother were safely away from the evil clutches of the Marcianos now and happily part of the Fitzfoster family.

'Too right! I've only just thawed out after our last adventure on ice!' Pippa said.

'Well, we'll just have to work a bit harder to find an adventure this time. There's got to be something. We're in London for goodness' sake!'

Suddenly there was a knock at the door and Linda Fitzfoster appeared carrying a huge box with feathers sticking out of it.

'Sorry to interrupt you, girls. I don't know if Molly

and Maria have told you, but we're having our annual summer party, which starts in our house but always ends in the residents' garden on Friday evening and it's tradition for us all to make our own hats for the infamous Fitzfoster headdress competition,' Linda said, placing the box on Molly's bed. 'Oh don't look like that, Maria. I know it's not your thing but I'm sure the others will help you come up with something wonderful,' she continued.

'Don't I usually?' Molly grinned.

Linda Fitzfoster made herself comfortable on the end of Molly's bed, going through every hat option, every silk flower, feather, and random decoration in the box. It was killing the girls. With Pippa only just having arrived, hats were the last thing they wanted to chat about. Maria and Molly were getting redder in the face with frustration by the second.

'Thanks, Mrs F,' Sally said, sensing someone ought to rescue the situation. 'We'll get started this afternoon. Pippa can't wait!'

Pippa felt a swift kick on her ankle. 'YELP! Erm . . . I mean yes, how exciting. I can't wait to get cracking. Is there a prize?'

'Ooooh yes – Mr Fitzfoster goes and buys the biggest box of chocolates he can find and the winner is presented with it at the end of the evening.'

'Great! Thanks, Mum. Errr, we were thinking of taking a picnic lunch to the square garden. Can we ask Mrs Dundas to rustle something up for us?' Maria said, thinking of somewhere they could go to be alone.

'Oh, yes, sure. Lovely idea. Take the blanket with the waterproof bottom though as the grass might be damp,' Linda Fitzfoster said, not realising she was being side-stepped.

'We will. The Sawyers are home now too, so we can see if they want to join us. See you at dinner!'

And with that, the girls ran down to the kitchen to beg for sandwiches and more flapjacks before making their way to the garden.

'Wow, this place is tidier than my bedroom!' Pippa said, looking around the immaculate lawns and flowerbeds.

'I know – isn't it lovely?' Molly said. 'It's only for the residents. Everyone living on the square has a key to the gate so they can come and go as they please, although I've never really seen anyone else use it.'

'Well you have now!' Danya shouted as she and Honey ran over from the opposite side of the garden, armed with a picnic basket.

'Great idea to meet out here, girls. Even though I'm not sure how good Greta's English is, it's still better to know she's not earwigging on our conversations,' Molly said.

'Tell us about it,' Maria groaned, remembering her mum's reluctance to leave them to it.

'Where shall we sit?' Danya asked, looking around.

'How about over by the fountain?' Pippa suggested, looking around the garden.

'Perfect! That's my favourite place too,' Honey answered.

As the girls laid out their blankets and began to see what goodies they'd been given for lunch, they started to have a proper catch-up.

'So how was Norfolk?' Sally asked.

'Well, funny you should ask but we did receive some rather big news,' Danya said.

'Good big news or bad big news?' Molly asked, gulping apple juice.

'We're not too sure how we feel about it yet,' Danya said.

'Oh, Dan, don't say that. It's lovely news. We just have to get used to the idea, that's all,' Honey said.

'What is it?' Maria asked.

'Mum's going to have a baby!' Honey blurted out.

'Wow. That is news. And I can see how that might come as a bit of a shock,' Maria said, wondering how she and Molly would take the news that they weren't about to be the only children in their parents' lives anymore.

'I think it's lovely. Just think, a new baby in the house to play with and dress up,' Molly said.

'Ha! Trust you,' Maria said gently.

'I think it's wonderful,' Pippa said, thinking how much she'd love a brother or sister. 'In fact I couldn't think of better news.'

'I agree,' Sally said. 'I think you girls forget how lucky you are to have each other sometimes. I would have loved to have someone to kick about with.'

'I think that's why we love you girls so much. You're the siblings we never had!' Pippa said.

'I'll drink to that!' Maria said, downing the rest of her juice.

'You're right. It will just take a bit of getting used to. Came as a bit of a shock, that's all,' Danya said.

'And what about your film, Molly – when's that out? I keep meaning to ask you,' Honey said.

'It's not out until the autumn. Gosh, how scary is that going to be, walking down the red carpet with all those cameras flashing?' Molly said.

'Oh awful! I can't imagine anything you'd hate more . . . Not!' Honey said and they all burst out laughing.

'Is that a statue of a ballerina on top of the fountain?' Pippa asked.

'Yes,' Molly said. 'Isn't she beautiful? I've often wondered if it's someone famous.'

'Most statues in London are of a well-known historical figure,' Danya said. 'Having lived on the square since we were born, I can't believe I've never thought to find out.'

'Me neither,' Maria said, on her feet and already prowling around the fountain for information.

'Over here!' Danya called from the other side. 'No wonder we never spotted it before.'

The girls ran round the fountain to where she was pointing at a very small metal plaque almost completely hidden at the stone base.

'It says . . . *In loving memory of Mina Elizabeth King 1828–blank*,' Danya said.

'What do you mean "blank"?' Maria said, having a look for herself.

'There's no second date. It's like they forgot to add the year that she died,' Danya said.

'That's weird, I thought people only erected memorial statues after someone had died – to remember them by. If that was the case, they'd have had the dates when they made the plaque. Why leave one off?' Pippa wondered.

The girls' heads were whirring with possibilities. It wasn't a particularly exciting mystery, but there was no doubt, it was a start.

'I'll look it up when we go home later,' Danya promised.

'Not if I find it first,' said Maria, giggling.

'Right – you're on!' Danya shouted and before the others could blink, Maria and Danya had darted back to their own houses to get a head start on their research.

'What are those two like . . . peas in a geeky pod!' Sally joked. 'More quiche anyone? Don't mind if I do!'

3

A Day of Discovery

Molly knew Maria would be up at the crack of dawn on *Gazette* Monday.

In an attempt to have a bit of a lie-in, she'd borrowed some earplugs and an eye-mask from her mum's bedside cabinet, which had worked a treat. But she had then spent the rest of the day feeling completely guilt-ridden that she hadn't gone to wave Maria off on her big day

'I can't bear it! What time is it now?' Molly asked for the four hundredth time that day.

'Coming up to six o'clock,' Sally said. 'She can't be much longer, can she? Don't grown-ups normally do nine till five at work?'

'I don't know, but she hasn't answered any of my texts,' Molly said, getting more wound up by the minute. 'I hope she's not upset I didn't wake up to wave her off. She must have been so hurt when she spotted me in Mum's eye-mask!'

'Don't be silly, Molly,' Pippa said. 'Maria wouldn't care about that. She'll have been like a ticking time-bomb this morning. All she would have thought about was not being late for her first day. And then she'll have been so focused once she got there, I bet she hasn't even had time to check her phone.'

'He-llllloooo!' came a bright and breezy voice from downstairs.

'Maria!' Molly squealed. If she could have slid all the way down the bannisters she would have.

'Oh Maria, how was it? I've been texting you all day. Are you all right?'

'Have you?' Maria said, looking quite the grown-up in her emerald top and carrying a business-like briefcase. 'Sorry, in my panic before I left this morning I totally forgot to take my phone off charge. It's still upstairs on silent,' Maria said, making a mental note to never ever do that again! She'd felt as though her left arm was missing, having spent the whole day without her mobile.

'How was it, Mimi?' came a booming voice from the sitting room.

Mr Fitzfoster, Story-seeker, was the only other person on the planet (apart from Molly) who dared refer to Maria as Mimi!

'Dad, it was awesome!' Maria exploded into her dad's arms. 'I learned so much. Thanks for letting me do it. It's everything I hoped for and more.'

Brian Fitzfoster smiled. He loved the passion in his girls. 'I think you'd better tell your sister all about it. She's been like a cat on hot coals all day waiting for you to come home.'

'Should have got up to wave me off this morning then, shouldn't you?' Maria winked at Molly. 'Only joking. I was pleased you were asleep. Sometimes you just have to be a complete stress-head on your own. No one and nothing could have calmed me down this morning. Actually nothing, that is, except the delicious cup of hot chocolate Dad's adorable driver, the ever-obliging Eddie gave me for the journey in to the Gazette. That did the trick. Blimey, I've got the chats haven't I? Come on girls, I'm starving – let's go down to the kitchen and I'll tell you all about it. Where are Dan and Honey?'

'They're not coming tonight. I think Greta's a bit stricter than they'd hoped!' said Pippa.

The girls listened intently as Maria proceeded to give a minute-by-minute account of her first day at the *Gazette*, in between mouthfuls of Mrs Dundas's deliciously cheesy lasagne.

'Hang on, first off, what was she wearing?' Molly asked, wondering about the great LT's wardrobe.

'I don't know. Prada?' Maria guessed, hoping she'd hit the mark.

'Perfect,' Molly said.

'So, we started the day in this big boardroom where LT holds a daily staff meeting, where they run through what stories they'll be following that day. Then at the end, she asked me which reporter I'd like to shadow!' Maria began.

'Really? How cool is that!' Sally said, imagining

herself dressed in a dark suit and crisp, white shirt, addressing a boardroom full of people.

'Yep. I picked this guy called Gareth Dawson. He was about to go to The Old George theatre to investigate some ghostly sightings . . .'

She was interrupted by a unanimous groan from the others, who'd all had quite enough of ghostly sightings following their run-in with Lucifette's fake ghost at L'Etoile.

'No honestly, this was real! I've never been into an empty theatre during the day – not a big London one anyway. It was as dark as when there's a performance and totally freezing, which Gareth said was a sign of ghostly activity. Anyway we sat in this box with a supernatural expert called Graham Buster who had all these machines with dials and pointers which started to go crazy after a while, meaning there was an actual ghost in the room . . .'

'There's no way I could have sat through that. I feel sick just thinking about it,' Molly said.

'Weren't you even a little bit scared?' Pippa asked.

'Of course I was,' Maria said. 'Terrified, but I couldn't show it or that might have been my first and last reporting job.'

'Hold on a second – did you just say the ghost guy

was called Graham Buster? As in G. Buster . . . as in Ghost Buster?' Sally stifled a laugh.

'Ha, Sally – you're brilliant. Honestly – comedy is in your blood. I'd never have picked up on that – remind me to email Gareth later. That's a cracking line for his article,' Maria said. 'But seriously, it was a brilliant day. Haven't had a second to check up on Mina Ballerina though. Anyone heard from Dan?'

'Not yet, so I don't suppose she's found anything on her either or she'd have been on the phone,' Pippa said.

Ring, ring, ring, ring.

'Talk of the devil!' Maria grinned, putting Danya and Honey on speaker, before telling them all about her day at the theatre. 'How about you guys? Have you been anywhere today?'

'You're joking aren't you? I haven't been able to prise Danya away from her laptop since she left the park yesterday. Nothing winds her up more than a dead end!' Honey said.

'I couldn't find anything yesterday afternoon either. I had hoped to poke about a bit at the *Gazette* today but just didn't get a chance. I'll try again tomorrow,' Maria said.

'Well, it hasn't all been fruitless,' Danya said.

'What? You mean while I've been stuck downstairs making German dumpling soup with Greta, you've been withholding important information?' Honey snapped.

'Shhhhh, Honey. I wanted to wait until we were all together. It could be something and it could be nothing,' Danya said.

'Go on . . .' Maria said softly.

'I've been thinking about the missing date and the most logical explanation is this. What if the death date is missing because the ballerina is missing?'

'Of course! The only way you'd have a memorial without a final resting date is if it was a mystery,' Maria said. 'Well done, Dan! I think you have something there.'

'This makes me think there must be something written about her somewhere in the *Gazette* archives. People don't just disappear without mention, especially if they are well known enough to be given a memorial statue. I'll find some excuse tomorrow to look in the archives,' Maria said.

'Great,' Danya answered.

'Girls, do you smell that?' Pippa asked with a twinkle in her eye.

'What?' asked Molly.

'The familiar scent of adventure!' she answered with a twinkle in her eye.

'And about time too!' Maria exclaimed. What a week this was shaping up to be!

4

Maria — Journaliste Extraordinaire

Luscious Tangerella, as it turned out,
Story-seeker, had anything but
a quiet morning planned for Maria.

'Maria! Great, you're early. You get extra points for punctuality at the *Gazette*. If there's one thing I can't stand it's a dawdler!'

Maria loved how LT launched into her day at a million miles an hour.

'Now, I have something extra special planned for you this morning if you're up to it?' LT continued, not really pausing for a response. 'We're off to Crabapple Dance Studios to meet with top music producer Phil

Goff, where he is auditioning for a new girl-band project he's putting together. As a L'Etoilette yourself, I'm sure you know more than me what this might entail.'

Wait until Pippa gets a load of this, Maria thought.

'He's on the hunt for a four-piece girl band to be the next big thing in pop and I have arranged for you to interview Phil, watch the auditions, and then briefly interview each girl as she comes off-stage. I thought with your young spin on this article, it might be a fresh angle for the *Gazette*. What do you say?'

Maria was aghast. 'You mean you actually want to publish me?'

'If it's good enough, Maria . . . sure, why not? You can't shadow at the *Gazette* without having an article published. 'Now let's shift . . . we're against the clock before we've even started today.'

'You're the best!' Maria exclaimed, quite forgetting herself.

'I know!' LT announced and swooshed off down the corridor in a manner that was more Madame Ruby than Madame Ruby.

While Maria was living the dream on one side of town, Molly, Pippa and Sally had been invited over to the Sawyers'. They'd already agreed they couldn't just rely on what Maria might find out but despite an entire morning spent trawling the internet on various computers, and even paying the fountain another visit, they hadn't come up with a single brainwave.

'Entshuldigung . . . sorry . . .' Greta appeared at the bedroom door. 'Lunch yes now? I vondered if you like grun salat mit chicken?'

The girls looked at each other blankly, but tried their best not to be rude.

'Yes please. That would be marvellous,' Sally said suddenly.

'Gut!' Greta continued in her best Germlish and left.

 (Germlish = German / English, Story-seeker)

'What did she just say?' Honey asked innocently. 'Honestly girls, you've no idea what we've been eating since we got back to London. We certainly haven't had a clue.'

'She's making chicken with green salad,' Sally said confidently.

'How in the world do you know that?' Molly asked.

'If you'd spent your whole life at the same school as Lucifette Marciano, you'd be good at foreign languages. If there was a class she wasn't interested in, you took it! She hated German, so I loved it. An hour of peace once a week, all to myself,' Sally said.

'Very impressive!' Danya said. 'Mind you, I'll tell you what's not impressive. Our dead-end, dead-beat investigating skills. I say we give up and do something fun this afternoon. Let's just hope Maria's had better luck at the Gazette than we have.'

'Good plan. Let's ask Greta if we can go bowling. There's a brilliant new place opened up that's just like an American diner, too. If this *grun salat*'s a bit limp, at least we can top up with a juicy burger and fries!' Honey said, her mouth watering at the thought.

'Great idea. I'll phone Mum and check she's OK with it,' Molly said and then separately under her breath, *Come on Maria, work some Maria-magic!*

Maria had had the time of her life, for the second day in a row. She felt like a top music journalist at LT's side and everyone was so nice to her, but she guessed that was what happened when you had the power of the printed word behind you. You could make or break careers at the touch of a button, and she loved every minute of it.

'My word, Maria. You're not finished already are you?' LT looked astounded as Maria's face appeared in the doorway not long after they got back to the office.

'It pretty much wrote itself, to be honest – it's such a great subject. I've called it "The Dream Maker".'

'Excellent header, Maria,' LT nodded approvingly. 'Did you get everything you needed?'

'And more! Mr Goff was very generous with his thoughts and information. In fact, I think I know exactly who's got the job, but I've made sure I keep everyone guessing in the article. It was so cool speaking to those girls. Each one was literally on the edge of their dreams, and hearing their advice about how to get there is definitely an experience I can take back to L'Etoile and share with the others,' Maria said, still buzzing.

'Once again, I applaud your dedication, Maria, and look forward to reading your copy. Why don't you go home early today? You've certainly earned it, bringing me that article in record time!' LT said.

'Actually, if you don't mind, I'd love a sneak peek into the *Gazette* archives. I keep walking past them. All that history at your fingertips!' Maria said as innocently as she could.

But LT wasn't born yesterday. 'Maria Fitzfoster, I do believe you're up to something and I like it! Help yourself, dear, and shout if you need anything. But remember one thing – make sure you give me the scoop on it, whatever it is you're snooping into, when you're ready.

'Will do,' Maria answered in shock.

That woman was even better than she thought! Boy, did she want to be the next Luscious Tangerella!

Maria sat down at the archive computer. The mere thought of how much knowledge she now had at her fingertips left her trembling with excitement.

Jack, the archive manager, had shown her how and where to access all the files. He told her that pretty much every *Gazette* article ever published was stored electronically, but if there was something in particular she was looking for it would always be worth double-checking the physical archive, all around them in the floor-to-ceiling filing cabinets.

For some, this might have been a bit challenging, but for the technical wiz that was Maria Fitzfoster, it took only seconds to locate the folder for articles from 1828, the starting point for her more detailed search for Mina Elizabeth King. She typed in ballet dancer, but nothing was coming up. She'd hoped that if there was something written about her disappearance, that would have been enough combined information to trigger a result. How annoying! She trawled through year after year but still didn't find anything. *Rats!* she thought. Maybe she'd have to ask LT whether she had a contact at the police who could look into their archives for missing-person reports. But what would that give her, apart from the devastating admission to LT that she'd hit a dead end before she'd really even started? She picked up the desk phone and called Molly.

'Hey, it's me . . . where are you?' Maria said in a whisper.

'At home with all the girls decorating our hats,' Molly said, putting her phone on speaker so the others could hear. 'Why? What's happening?'

'Absolutely nothing!' Maria said. 'I can't bear it.

I've checked everything I can think of but there's not a single mention of our missing ballerina . . . anywhere.'

'Oh no! What are we going to do?' Molly said.

'Do you reckon you girls can go back to the fountain and have another look? We simply must be missing something. I refuse to give up. There has to be more.'

'No probs. The girls and I were just saying that,' Molly said.

'It's possible we missed something, I suppose,' Danya answered. 'We didn't look that closely before, did we?'

'Even if we can find out who commissioned the statue in the first place. That might at least give us another name to research,' Maria said.

'We're on it! Call you back, Mimi,' Molly said.

'Yes – but on this office number,' Maria said quickly. 'Has it come up on your phone? I've got no signal in here. Must be the walls of newspapers around me blocking it.'

As the girls approached the fountain, the stone ballerina on top looked more beautiful and mysterious than ever against the bluest of skies.

'Come on girls, I've got a good feeling about this,' Pippa said.

'Me too. Spread out around the fountain and let your fingers run over every inch of the stone. There's years of dirt and growth over it and we mustn't miss anything this time,' Danya instructed.

Twenty minutes passed as the five girls felt every lump and bump on the fountain, before Pippa suddenly called out in excitement.

As the others approached, she was crouched down in front of the date plaque they'd found originally.

'Supercalifragilisticexpialidocious!' she cried. 'How could we have got that so wrong?'

'Did she just say . . . ?' Honey said, smothering a giggle at Pippa's outburst.

'Don't ask!' Sally said. 'She's a modern-day Mary Poppins apparently and that's just what she says when she doesn't know what else to say. You'll get used to it!'

'Pippa, you are hilar—' Honey started before she was interrupted by Molly.

'Erm, Pippa, I hate to say it, but that's the same plaque we found yesterday,' Molly said, teasing.

'Erm, Molly. I know! But have a closer look and tell me how on earth we didn't spot that!'

'Spot what?' Honey said, trying to squeeze in.

'Pippa, you're a genius!' Danya exclaimed. 'I'll let you do the honours and tell the others or we'll be here all day.'

'Look closely at the date – the first 8 isn't an eight at all! It's a nine! There's just a curvy scratch right across it which makes it look like an eight,' Pippa said, triumphantly.

'You mean all this time we've been looking at the wrong century?' Molly said, flabbergasted.

'Right! Mina was born in 1928, a whole hundred years after we started looking!' Danya said.

'Oooooh, well done Pippa,' Molly said, picking up her phone. 'This has got to make a difference to Mimi's search.' 'Mimi, you were right. But it was something we got wrong, not something new. The plaque was so badly scratched we read it wrong. Her date of birth isn't 1828 but 1928!' Molly squealed.

'You're joking! I knew it! There had to be something else. When are our lives ever simple? Well done, peeps. I'll get right on it,' Maria said and hung up.

'I'm going home to see what I can do with the new date,' Danya announced. 'You coming, Hon?'

'Actually I think I might stay here with the others; three's a crowd when you're with your laptop!' Honey grinned.

'OK, cool. I'll come over in an hour or so – hopefully with some exciting news for a change!'

5

Eureka!

Maria was mumbling with her head in her hands when the manager, Jack, came back to check on her.

'Can I help, Maria? It's usually the filing I find frustrating, never the research,' he said, trying to lift her spirits.

'Oh, hi, Jack. I'm sorry. I've just been hitting wall after wall with this case and can't seem to catch a break,' Maria said, talking like some police detective.

'I see. And you've tried searching the physical archive too?' Jack asked, feeling sorry for her.

'Three times!' Maria answered.

'I see. Right. Well, there's only one other place where you might find what you're looking for . . . if it exists that is,' Jack said thoughtfully.

'Yes?' Maria said, jumping up.

'The unpublished archive. It's still on the computer, but in a different folder. Look, I'll show you,' Jack said, tapping away until the file popped up. 'Try putting your search words in here and see if you find anything. If it's not there . . . then it's not anywhere!'

He smiled and turned to go.

'Thanks so much!' Maria said. 'Can I just ask one more thing, though? Why would there be any unpublished articles anyway? Surely everything would get printed at some point, even if things had to be put on the back burner for a while.'

'Yes, that's a good point. The only way I can see a subject being dropped is if it put someone, or something, at risk. Even journalists have a heart, you know,' he said and left.

Maria sat for a moment, thinking about that. Was there a chance that poor Mina's life had been at risk? *The plot thickens*, she thought. *Oh please let there be something here.*

She hadn't even finished typing in Mina's full name

when the search result screen popped up with ONE result in the box.

'Yesssss!' she hissed to herself as she clicked through to an article dated 29 September 1944, entitled 'Mystery of the Missing Ballerina, by Horatio Tangerella'.

Maria gasped as she read out the journalist's name.

'Horatio Tangerella?' she muttered out loud. 'Has to be a relative of LT, maybe even her father! Yes, that would make sense with the date. WATC?'

She scrolled down to the article:

Police have this evening confirmed that they have no leads regarding the sudden disappearance of Mina Elizabeth King. Most readers will not yet be familiar with the name, but Miss King was poised to become one of England's most exciting ballet debuts before she mysteriously disappeared on Sunday evening. At sixteen years old, she was about to become the youngest ever ballerina on the Sadler's Wells ballet tour, starring alongside Margot Fonteyn. Why should a girl with such a star-lit future suddenly disappear from the face of the planet? Why did she fail to arrive for her first ever professional stage appearance? Was she kidnapped? Did she run away? Is she alive, or is she dead? One thing for certain is that nothing is for certain. The search goes on for any clues and Miss King's father, Mr Charles King, is helping the police with their enquiries . . .

Maria had almost forgotten to take a breath and suddenly gasped for air. Finally! she thought. But why on earth was this article never published? Surely any publicity would have helped to find Mina? Particularly if her picture was splashed across all of the newspapers.

As she scrolled down further there was a photograph of the young, beautiful, brunette ballerina as she posed for her first press shots. There she was, striking a pirouette-type pose in a tutu, which immediately reminded Maria of their own fountain statue. Further down there was another photo, of a dark haired-man in a suit, standing on some very grand black and white chequered steps.

'Her poor father,' Maria muttered, thinking what her own father would do if she or Molly disappeared. Suddenly she spotted something and stood up to lean into the screen as closely as possible.

'Jackpot!' she squealed for the second time that

afternoon. But it wasn't the man she was focusing on, it was the house in the background and the number on the door. Forty-five. She'd recognise those chequered tiles anywhere.

Time to get home to the others!

6

A Secret Revealed

'No, look closer!' Maria said to Danya after they'd all read the article. 'The picture of her dad, look where he is.'

'No way!' Danya exclaimed suddenly. 'But that's . . .'

'Next door!' Honey cried.

'Exactly. It would seem that Mina Ballerina lived with her father at forty-five Beaufort Square. So she might not even have made it as far as the theatre that night. It might all have happened right here, in our very own back garden,' Maria said.

Everyone fell silent, imagining the worst of what might have happened to poor Mina.

Mrs Dundas appeared in the doorway.

'Sorry to interrupt you ladies, but Greta's come to take Danya and Honey home.'

'No way! How embarrassing! Doesn't she realise we're old enough to walk to the other side of the square by ourselves?' Danya moaned.

'That's what Mina said,' Sally said.

'Oh don't!' Molly answered, cringing.

'Actually,' Mrs Dundas said, 'it was really rather considerate of her. It's raining cats and dogs out there so she's brought the car around for you.'

'Is it?' Maria said, running to the window. 'When did that happen? It wasn't raining when I drove home.'

'Haven't you seen the news? There's a bad storm coming in this evening and by the looks of it, it's brewing quite nicely,' Mrs Dundas said.

'OK. Thanks Mrs D,' Molly said. 'They're coming now. See you tomorrow my lovelies!'

That night saw the most horrendous summer thunderstorm to hit London for years.

Torrential rain gushed along the roads and

pavements. Everyone was awake practically the entire night listening to the chaos outside and, in the Sawyers' case, the chaos inside. Poor Greta had spent the whole night in the cellar with the Sawyers' housekeeper, Mrs Worsley, emptying buckets of water, as rainwater poured in.

'Poor things. We offered to help but they sent us back up to bed. As if we could sleep anyway,' Honey said on the phone to Molly the following morning. 'The rain was so loud on the roof, it was like sleeping in a tent!'

'Why don't we come over in a bit to help – we could offer to give Greta and Mrs Worsley a rest while we take over. Bet they won't say no this time! They'll be exhausted by now,' Molly said.

'Really? That would be fantastic. Has Maria gone already?' Honey asked.

'Yes, she had to get up even earlier than usual this morning as she's off to the city to climb the Shard – whatever that is! It's up to us today to follow up on the lead about your next-door neighbour.'

'Even more reason to come over to us then! We could use the flood as an excuse to knock and see who lives there. You know, pretend we're checking they're all right. Mind you, I'm not sure anyone

lives there. I've never seen anyone go in or out!'
Honey said.

'Great – see you in a min then,' Molly said, hanging
up.

♡

Danya couldn't help but burst into giggles when she
opened the front door and faced Molly, Pippa and
Sally in full wet-weather gear from head to toe.

'What do you think this is? Auditions for *Singing in
the Rain*? Have you looked in the mirror, Molly? I'm
surprised at you!' Danya said.

'Needs must when you're battling the elements,
Danya, dear,' Molly joked. Besides, she was more
worried about getting her newly blow-dried hair
wet than what she looked like from the neck
down.

'You might as well keep it all on if we're going
straight down to the cellar. It's wetter down there
than it is outside!' Honey said, secretly chuffed her
waterproofs and wellies were far more fashionable
than theirs.

'I think it's safe to say that the Sawyers haven't had
much luck with water leaks lately, what with poor
Grandma and now us, here,' Danya said.

'Wow, I can't believe we didn't have any leaks,' Molly said, looking at the flooding as they walked down the dark cellar steps.

'Yours has probably been reinforced and redecorated recently. I don't think our cellar has been touched since the day we moved in,' Honey said, reaching for a light cord above her head.

'Nooooooo!' Danya shrieked. 'You'll electrocute us all!'

Honey was mortified. 'Of course! Water and electricity don't mix. How could I have been so stupid?'

Danya opened the big bag of tricks she'd brought with her and started dealing out torches. Never had she looked so like Maria! As they shone them around the cellar, they saw rolled up soggy blankets and buckets everywhere.

'Poor Mrs Worsley and Greta!' Pippa said, imagining a whole night of mopping up sludgy water.

'Luckily it's mostly wine stored down here, and that won't get damaged by water,' Danya said, shining her torch over the racks of once dusty, now glistening bottles.

'That may be true, but what about our old toy trunk!' Honey said, racing over to a large navy-blue trunk with a rusty catch.

'That should be all right,' Pippa said. 'My uncle Harry's got one similar in his studio that he keeps all his old vinyl records in and that never let water in when the shed roof leaked.'

'It's pouring in over here,' Molly said, watching rain trickling down the wall like a mini-waterfall.

'Yes, that's the side which faces the street – so it's just running in from the pavement,' Honey said, coming over to have a look.

Danya grabbed a mop and as she started to swish it through the water, she noticed something strange.

'That's a bit odd,' she said, shining her beam across the floor. 'Look, the water's running away somehow. It's coming down the wall, running along the flagstones straight under our trunk and then disappearing.'

'What's so weird about that?' Molly asked, confused.

'Well, by rights, with this much water coming in, it should be waist-high by now. Listen . . .'

Everyone fell silent. All they could hear was the gurgle of water draining away.

'There must be a drain or something under the trunk!' Sally said. 'How lucky is that! Whatever's

♥ 53 ♥

under there has stopped your cellar from filling up completely!'

'Let's have a look, shall we? Give me a hand, Sal,' Danya said, passing Honey her torch.

Piled on top of the toy trunk were two old tea-chests so after Sally and Molly had shifted those to one side, Pippa and Danya heaved the huge trunk away from the wall.

'OMG!' Honey and Molly said, staring at a man-sized circular grille in the cellar wall.

All five torches were suddenly pointing at it, revealing a long dark tunnel behind.

'Supercala . . .' Pippa started.

'. . . fragilisticexpialidocious!' the others joined in.

Danya grabbed her bag from the cellar steps, pulled out a selection of screwdrivers and chisels and immediately began hacking away at the grille bolts.

'Bingo-bango!' she called as the last bolt came free. Pippa helped her to roll the grille to one side and the five girls stood looking into the mouth of the blackest tunnel they had ever seen.

'I can't believe this! And in our house too!' Honey said.

'How could Mum and Dad not know about this?' Danya asked, hardly believing what she was seeing.

'You don't know they don't!' Sally answered. 'If you had a dark tunnel under your house, leading to who knows where, would you tell your children about it?'

'What do we do, then? What if Mrs Worsley comes down and sees it?' Honey said.

'We lock the cellar door while we investigate and deal with the consequences later if she comes looking for us,' Danya said, running up the cellar steps.

'Right then. Ladies first,' Danya said, motioning to Honey and Molly to lead the way.

'Not a chance. You first, Dan!' replied Honey. 'This is your little discovery.'

'Fine, follow me and stay close. We don't want anyone disappearing on us!'

'Ha! Ha! Very funny,' Molly said sarcastically.

Once they were about four metres away from the entrance, the tunnel suddenly opened up and was surprisingly wide and tall, with more than enough space for the five girls to walk alongside each other. What's more, the walls appeared to have been tiled.

'It feels a bit like we're on the London Underground!' Pippa said.

'Yes!' Danya agreed. 'That's exactly what it feels like.'

'It's a good job Maria isn't with us. Don't you remember how claustrophobic she got in the Wilton smugglers' cave!' Molly said.

'Well, let's just hope we don't meet with any fast-moving headlights!' said Sally.

'Oh don't. Can you imagine if we've somehow linked up with the Tube network,' Honey said.

'I don't think we have to worry about that,' Danya said, seeing the end of the tunnel ahead.

The girls suddenly found themselves in the most enormous space. It was the size of a netball court with openings leading off all around. It was surprisingly airy for somewhere buried so deep underground, but a musty smell hung in the atmosphere, a bit like an old compost heap.

'Would you just look at this place! A maze of secret tunnels right under our square!' gasped Honey, in awe.

'Fifty more tunnels like ours, you mean,' Danya

said. 'Each one leading to another house on the square.'

'No way!' Molly said, open-mouthed.

'I know what it is!' said Pippa, jumping up and down. 'I've read about places like this. They're called bomb shelters. They were built and used during the war so that people had somewhere safe to go when there were bombs going off above ground.'

'How incredible!' Sally said, looking around.

'Look at that,' said Honey, pointing to a large dusty table, covered in rusty old tins and paper.

'Wow, I wouldn't fancy putting this corned beef in a sandwich,' Sally said, picking up a tin where the label had almost flaked off entirely with age. 'It must be at least sixty years old.'

'A teddy!' Molly said, making out a grubby, fluffy face propped up against one of the table legs.

'What is this place?' Honey asked, sifting through a box of yellowed books.

'All the residents in the square must have clubbed together to have this shelter built to protect their families during the war,' Danya said, as she picked up an old gas mask, the sort of thing everyone had in case of a gas attack.

'That's so cool. I saw one of those in the war museum last year when Mum took me,' Sally said.

'Hold on a sec . . . rewind. Are you saying one of these tunnels runs directly to our cellar too?' asked Molly.

'I reckon so, yes. But I wouldn't like to hazard a guess as to which. Even if you counted round to number seven, we can't be sure it's yours. The only way to know for sure is to have a look in your cellar and see if we can find an entrance like ours,' Danya said.

'Oh my gosh! How exciting is this? You know what this means, girls?' Molly squealed. 'We can meet up whenever we like – secretly – without our parents knowing we've even left the house! Maria is going to pop when she hears about this!'

'We'd best be getting back in case Greta's trying to get into the cellar. They'll think we've drowned or something,' Honey said quickly.

'Cool. I'll just take a few pics of our new Adventure HQ to show Maria. It's probably too dark but she'll get the general idea,' Molly said.

'Oh no!' Sally said in a panic as they turned to leave only to be faced with a wall of identical tunnels. 'How do we know which one we just came through? They all look the same!'

'Amateurs, girls, amateurs!' Danya said as she marched directly into the tunnel she'd chalked a big

'S' for Sawyer into when they'd arrived, for exactly that reason.

'Dan! You're so clever. Maria had better watch out!' Molly giggled and the girls disappeared back along the tunnel, eager to find out whether the Fitzfosters' cellar was as exciting!

7

Adventure HQ

By the time Molly, Pippa and Sally arrived home, it was long past lunchtime and Linda Fitzfoster was starting to feel a little concerned as to where the girls had got to. She'd been hoping to join them all for the lovely lunch Mrs Dundas had made and started to panic when she couldn't reach of any of them on their mobiles.

Of course she couldn't,
Story-seeker . . . one's phone doesn't work
a million miles underground!

'Sorry we're late, Mrs F! We just lost all track of time,' Sally said, sheepishly.

'Yes, sorry, Mum. You know what we're like when we all get together, tunnel vision!' Molly said.

Pippa and Sally tried hard to smother their giggles.

'It's just been so lovely to have the run of the square,' Pippa said. 'I've led such a sheltered life.'

Molly nearly spat out her four-cheese tortellini.

'I just love it when we all sit down and eat as a family. It's really something worth cellar-brating!' Sally said and burst out laughing.

'What on earth has got into you today?' Linda Fitzfoster asked. 'You're behaving very strangely indeed.'

The girls immediately tried their best to be serious. No more jokes.

'Now listen,' Linda continued. 'Don't forget that your dad and I have to leave this afternoon for the Dublin Diamond Conference, but we'll be back around midday tomorrow. Mrs Dundas is in charge so please do everything she says and don't get up to any mischief!'

'Don't sweat it, Mum,' Molly said. 'It's not like someone's about to drop a bomb on the square or anything!'

And with that the girls completely lost the plot. They were hysterical.

'Right. I'll see you in the morning,' Linda said. 'Good luck, Mrs Dundas. I fear you're going to need it with these loopy girls today.'

Mrs Dundas had never seen the girls eat so fast as when Mrs Fitzfoster left the room.

'Would you like some cheesecake?' she said as they started to stand up.

'Maybe later, thanks, Mrs D,' Molly said. 'I'm absolutely stuffed!'

'Me too,' Pippa groaned with indigestion.

'OK well, mind you don't leave the house this afternoon, girls. Your parents have left me in charge and my heart won't take you doing a disappearing act on me!' Mrs Dundas pleaded.

'We absolutely promise we won't step foot out of the front door until Mum and Dad are back. How's that, Mrs D?' Molly said with a knowing grin. 'In fact I thought I might go through some of our old stuff in the cellar this afternoon. There's some old art work I'd love to show the others,' she said, delighted with her cunning plan.

'Excellent,' Mrs Dundas said, relieved to have control of the situation.

'In fact, Mrs D, why don't you take your coffee to the sitting room and have a rest. You haven't stopped today and if it's just us here now and we promise not to make a mess, there'll be very little to do before Mum and Dad get back tomorrow. We'll even clear away the lunch things,' Sally said, doing her bit to ensure Mrs D was as far away from the cellar as possible.

'Oh, how kind of you. And to think I was so worried you might be up to your old tricks. I wouldn't mind a little sit down, to be honest. My knee's been playing up again this week. Thank you very much. Just call if you need me,' Mrs D said before disappearing up the stairs.

The girls left it as long as possible before bursting out laughing.

'Oh my days, Moll. When you said tunnel vision, I thought my sides were going to split!' Sally said. 'That was the funniest lunch I've ever sat through!'

'What a team!' Molly said. 'We've managed to shore up Mrs D for at least a couple of hours. The poor dear's that tired, she'll be snoring in seconds.'

'Right then,' Pippa said. 'I'll nip up and check your parents have gone and see if the Dundas coast is clear. I want to grab something from the study anyway. Meet you in the cellar in five.'

And as Pippa ran upstairs, Sally looked at Molly quizzically. 'Something from the study?'

'No idea. Come on. Let's get these bowls in the dishwasher. I want to have the maximum possible to tell Maria when she gets back.'

Sally had never seen such an organised cellar. Only the Fitzfosters would have somewhere as organised as this. Even the lighting was brilliant. No wonder this place hadn't flooded.

Pippa closed the cellar door behind her.

'Wow!' she said as she took in the walls of cabinets and built-in storage. 'Is everything in your house labelled?'

'Where do you think Mimi gets it from?' Molly said. 'Mum's just as OCD. Between them, they could locate every lost thing on planet earth if they put their minds to it.'

(OCD = Obsessive Compulsive
Disorder, Story-seeker)

Finally, Pippa thought. *An abbreviation I've heard of!*

'What's in the bag, Pips?' Sally asked, spotting the rucksack Pippa had slung over her shoulder.

'Ah ha! A little stroke of genius on my part. Our phones might not get any signal down here, but these just might,' she said and pulled out their old walkie-talkie watches.

'Didn't we leave these at Wilton?' Sally said.

'We did, but I remembered overhearing Maria ask Mrs Dundas to put them all on charge in the study before the storm. Just in case communications went down. She must have got Eddie to pick them up or something,' Pippa answered.

'Well done the pair of you. Let's just hope they work,' Molly said, twisting the dials on each unit to the same channel to link them up.

'Testing . . . testing . . . one, two . . .' Sally said in a deep voice. Straight away her voice echoed in the other watches. 'Working perfectly! Brilliant!'

'Come on then. It's time to find out whether there's a Fitzfoster tunnel, or all of this will be useless anyway,' Pippa said.

The girls turned again to look at the room. The problem was, all of the storage had been built in properly. If there was a tunnel opening to number seven Beaufort Square, there was every chance it had been blocked up. They began to move around the room, tugging at the units to see if any pulled away, but without luck.

'It's hopeless,' Molly said, slumping on the floor. 'We can't very well start smashing up all the cabinets to see what's behind, can we? How would we explain that one?'

Pippa gave Molly's shoulder a squeeze.

'Maybe we don't have to!' Sally said thoughtfully.

Molly jumped up.

'What's the one thing in this cellar which shouldn't be here?' Sally said.

Pippa and Molly followed her gaze. She wasn't looking at any of the cabinets. She was looking at a wooden fireplace which had been boarded up.

'Why would you have a boarded up fireplace?' Sally asked, scrambling in a drawer marked TOOLS to her right.

'Oh my goodness, she's right. You'd only block it up if it didn't work, or to stop any drafts,' Pippa said.

'Or . . .' Sally said as she loosened the last screw

holding the surround to the wall, 'if you wanted to hide a secret tunnel behind!' She grinned as the board came away in one piece, revealing a familiar-looking grille behind.

'Sally, you did it! Well done!' Molly shrieked. 'I'm nipping up to text Honey and Danya we're on our way while you two get the grille off. Back in two.'

At forty-four Beaufort Square, Danya and Honey had been quizzing Mrs Worsley about their mystery neighbour.

'Honestly, I've not seen anyone come and go for years, but the house is definitely still occupied as every so often I hear a hoover or music through the walls. You should speak to Peter. He knows everything about everyone on the square,' Mrs Worsley said.

'Peter?' Honey asked. 'Who's Pet—'

'The postman,' Danya said quickly. 'Great idea, Mrs Worsley. Don't know why we didn't think of that!'

'Why the sudden interest in number forty-five anyway? What's going on?' Mrs Worsley asked.

'Oh nothing – we were just wondering whether

their cellar might have flooded and how damaging that could be if the house was empty,' Danya answered.

'How thoughtful of you,' Mrs Worsley said, smiling at the twins.

See how quick-minded our L'Etoilettes are, Story-seeker. An answer, or a little white lie, for everything . . . well, only for a good cause, that is.

Beep, beep. Honey's phone sounded.

'They've found it, Dan!' she whispered excitedly. 'They're in!'

'Then we're on!' Danya answered and as soon as Mrs Worsley took the ironing upstairs, they ran down to the cellar, squeezed behind the trunk and felt their way along the dark, murky tunnel to meet their friends.

'Molly . . . Pippa . . . Sal . . . you guys there?' Honey called as they reached the middle. Not having a clue from which tunnel the others were about to come, they stood in the silence, listening to their own heartbeats pound with excitement.

Suddenly the beam from a torch shone out, followed by three whispering girls.

'We made it!' Sally said, proud of her handiwork in locating the Fitzfoster tunnel.

'Can you believe this is happening?' Molly said. 'Maria is going to be so impressed when we show her what we've found. I'm not even going to show her the photos I took. We'll surprise her with it in the flesh!'

The others couldn't wait to see the look on Maria's face. They'd come so far in such a short time, and what a find!

'Here, take these,' Pippa said, handing the Sawyers Maria's walkie-talkie watch. The others would just have to share theirs between them. 'We've checked they work underground and they do.'

'Coooool!' Honey breathed. 'I've always wanted to have a go on these. How do you work it?'

While Molly gave Honey a quick lesson, Danya chalked up a big F at the mouth of the Fitzfosters' tunnel, so they knew how to get back.

'Look, why don't we come back again tonight and bring Maria? The fact that the tunnels open right up after the first few metres should keep her claustrophobia at bay. We'll just keep her talking for the first bit. I think we had better go home now. It took us a bit longer to find our tunnel so I'm worried Mrs D might be up and about again,' Honey said.

'No probs. Just radio us when you're ready!' Honey said, holding her watch up to her mouth like a secret agent.

'Ha! We will. Be ready for us!' Molly said, and the girls disappeared into their respective tunnels.

8

Maria's Underground Tour

'Maria! What time is it? Have you only just got back?' Molly said, waking up suddenly.

Maria arrived home as the girls were having supper, jubilant after another fabulous day in the world of hot-shot journalism. She'd spent the day at London's tallest building, the Shard, watching a man climb all the way down the outside, without a safety harness, for charity. The man was a bit bonkers but it was for such a great cause. He was as selfless as he was crazy and that made him a hero in Maria's eyes.

Molly had been trying to get a word in edgeways, but it was as if Maria was in some kind of a story-telling trance and it was impossible to get her attention without sharing their mischief with Mrs Dundas too.

'MA-RIA!' Molly exploded as Mrs Dundas finally finished her supper and left the girls to it.

Maria jumped out of her skin. 'What!' she said in a panic. The look of frustration on her sister's face said it all. 'Oh my goodness, what have you found? I've been like a whirlwind, haven't I?'

'Shhhhhhhh!' Molly, Sally and Pippa all hissed at once.

Maria fell silent, and watched in surprise as Pippa pulled out a walkie-talkie watch and spoke.

'Camp forty-four, this is Camp seven, are you receiving, over?

'Loud and clear. Go ahead, Camp seven,' came Danya's voice.

Maria gasped and grinned. *What had this little lot been up to today?*

'We're going in, Camp forty-four. Repeat, Camp seven is going in. See you in five, over,' Pippa finished.

Molly ran around the kitchen table and pulled Maria's chair out with her still on it. 'Come on, sis. Time to be wowed!'

Maria was trembling with excitement. It wasn't often that she was the last to know about something and she was enjoying the anticipation. She followed the girls down the cellar stairs and across to where the old fireplace was now just propped up against a cabinet.

'Oh...my...stars...' Maria said slowly as she stared at the grille and the tunnel behind it. Immediately her hands started to get clammy and her head began to swim with fear. *Get a grip, Maria!* she told herself. 'In there?' she said.

'Yep!' Molly said, spotting Maria's panic. 'It's fine, Mimi, I promise. It opens up into a huge space almost as soon as you get in.'

'Follow us!' Sally said, grabbing Maria's hand. 'You won't believe it!'

As they trotted into the bomb shelter for the third time that day, the atmosphere was electric.

'Maria!' Danya and Honey exclaimed when they spotted the others.

Maria had never been so relieved to be out of that tunnel and felt immediately better as she looked at the space around her.

'What? But how?' Maria stammered, trying to work it all out. 'Don't tell me you've got one of these tunnels too?'

'Exactamundo!' Danya said. 'And from the looks of this place – so have most of the other houses on the square!'

Maria stared, utterly speechless as she shone her torch beam around the enormous room, seeing tunnel after tunnel.

'This is crazy,' she said. 'How did you even find this place?'

The girls took it in turns to run through their day and how one discovery had led to another.

'We're just lucky that storm hit last night. If Danya and Honey's cellar hadn't leaked, we'd never have found it,' Sally said.

'I can't believe it's still raining! Just listen to it. Sounds like the whole ceiling's about to cave in,' Honey said.

'That's not rain!' Maria announced, thoughtfully. 'We must be right under the fountain!'

'Of course! You're right. This place is enormous. It makes complete sense for it to run the whole length of the residents' garden,' Sally said, looking up.

'My goodness, yes, the fountain! This would all have definitely been here in Mina Ballerina's day. If this was built during the war it would definitely have existed when she lived on the square,' Molly said, suddenly remembering the missing girl and connecting the dots. 'Would have been a very handy way for a kidnapper to come and go with her without being seen.'

'Or for her to escape. I've been thinking about Horatio's article. Maybe she couldn't face a life in the spotlight and decided to make a run for it before going on tour,' Pippa said.

'But isn't that exactly the sort of life all ballet dancers dream of – a life in the spotlight? I certainly would if I was Mina,' Honey said.

'Hmmm. None of this makes any sense. Nor does it explain why the article was never published. Where would the risk be in printing a story about a kidnap or a disappearance? Surely it would have helped the family to find her if it had been printed,' Danya said.

'Not if Mina's father respected his daughter's wishes enough to let her go and live the life she wanted to. He would have had enough money to pay Horatio not to print the story, surely?' Pippa said.

'I don't buy it,' Maria said. 'I think poor Mina's disappearance was much more suspicious than that. There's no way a member of the Tangerella family would take a bribe not to print something. There must have been some reason, a risk for Mina that simply wasn't worth taking. Either way, there has to be another way out to the square other than all of these residents' tunnels.'

'What?' the others looked at Maria, confused. They'd all thought each of the tunnels led to a different house.

'Think about it. Whoever designed this bomb shelter would have put in an exit to the street somewhere, just in case all of the houses were levelled,' Maria said.

Straight away, Danya started trying to picture if there was anything on the square or in the garden which might conceal another entrance.

'We could go off in pairs taking a tunnel at a time and see whether any lead outside,' said Honey.

'You'd have thought any tunnel to the open air would have such a draft coming down it, it would be easy to spot,' Molly said.

'Not if it's blocked up from the outside, Mol. I'm not suggesting for a second it's going to be that easy to locate,' Maria said. *When is anything easy?*

'Let's split up then,' Danya said. 'Honey and I will start working our way round from this tunnel to the right. Sal, you and Pippa do the same but go left – and you Fitzfosters pick a tunnel on the other side of the shelter and we'll all keep going until we meet up. And for goodness' sake remember to chalk up the tunnel you start in, so we know when we're back to the start.'

Danya handed out different-coloured chalks from her tunnel-marking chalk pack and made a start. This was going to take a little while but they were ready for the challenge, each pair secretly hoping they'd be the ones to discover the outside exit – not that they were even sure there was one at this point!

'Sa-lly! Pi-ppa! We've reached your starting point and found nothing,' Molly called, spotting a big yellow chalk cross on the wall where Pippa and Sally's search had begun. Maria was too frustrated to talk.

Sally and Pippa went to try a tunnel at the north side of the shelter. 'Find anything?' Sally called back.

'Nothing! Just a load of boarded up tunnels with grilles identical to the ones in our cellar and the Sawyers'. We reckon they're all residents' tunnels,' Molly shouted back. 'You?'

'We're the same. Nothing out of the ordinary – but I can see Dan and Honey's blue cross after the next tunnel so we've got one more to check,' Pippa said.

Danya and Honey exited their last tunnel, having arrived at Molly and Maria's number one.

'What a waste of time!' said Danya, feeling exasperated. 'I was so sure we were going to find something. Not even the hint of a draft or daylight!'

'Daylight would have been a miracle, Dan, given that it's dark outside now!' said Honey, giggling.

'I feel your pain, Danya,' Maria said. 'Maybe they are all residents' tunnels. It was just an idea. What about the one next to yours? Do you think that leads to forty-five?' Maria asked.

'It's hard to tell, but the good news is that it's not boarded up at all! You just can't see into the cellar because there's something been pushed up against it the other side. So if we take the grille off, we can definitely have a peek about in their cellar if we want to,' Danya said.

'Peek about?' Molly exclaimed. 'Peek about? I don't think the police would refer to it as a peek about! More like breaking and entering. Have you completely lost the plot?'

'Molly's right. We can't go breaking into someone's house – even if we think we have the best reason in the world. Mina Ballerina is hardly going to be hiding out in the cellar of her own house, is she, and even if she was, I'm not sure I'd like to see her!' Honey said, her imagination running wild.

'Calm down you two,' Maria coaxed. 'We're not going to do anything rash. Dan, didn't you say something about the postman? Why don't you guys try that route tomorrow, see if we can't get into forty-five through the front door, like any normal person.'

Molly and Honey looked relieved.

Suddenly, they heard muffled shrieks and steps running from the end of the shelter.

Sally and Pippa appeared, panting, but delighted.

'We think we might have something. Come see, come see!' Sally called.

Maria, Molly, Honey and Danya ran to join them.

'See anything weird?' Pippa said, as they walked along.

'Not when you take into account that there are about fifty other long dark tunnels around here, that look just the same,' Molly joked.

They shone their torches into the gloom.

'Not exactly the same, Molly!' Maria said, feeling relieved as she spotted stone steps at the end of yet another dark, dingy tunnel!

'Dan, why didn't we think of that? Of course there had to be steps up! How else would you get to street level!'

'It's so obvious now you think about it,' Danya said. 'In our cellar entrances, you go up the cellar steps to ground level. If this exit goes to the street, there had to be steps up from the tunnel itself!'

As they neared the top step, they could see another grille, boarded from the other side.

'Feel! Feel around the edge. That's too cold to be coming from anyone's cellar. I can even hear a car!' Pippa said.

'Well done, girls. All we have to do now is find this entrance from the outside,' Molly said.

'That's going to be easy – NOT!' Sally said. 'It's just taken us an hour and a half to find it from this side.'

'Look, let's think about this logically,' said Maria. 'Dan, would you say this tunnel is roughly halfway between your tunnel and ours?'

'Yep,' Danya said, taking over. 'And if your house and ours are roughly in the middle of the street either side of the garden, this tunnel must lead out at one end of the square.'

'Right!' Maria said. 'And if there's a row of houses one end and a church with plenty of ground around it at the other, I know where I'd start!'

'The church!' Molly exploded.

'Oh great,' Honey groaned. 'Nothing I'd like better than a little expedition through a graveyard in the dead of night.'

'Don't be daft, sis. We're not doing it now . . . are we?' Danya said, looking at Maria.

'No chance. I'm exhausted and have another early start tomorrow. You girls can make this your morning mission. What a terrific find!' Maria said with a yawn, pleased to have a day off tunnelling underground.

'See you in the morning then. Radio us when you're ready,' Pippa said.

'Night!' they called and ran home to bed.

9

Number Forty-Five Beaufort Square

'Shouldn't we wait for the others?' Honey said as she and Danya stood on the steps of forty-five Beaufort Square.

'We're just going to knock. Like we said to Mrs W, we're being neighbourly, calling in to check whether they're having any flood problems and need help,' Danya said.

Knock, knock. The rapping seemed to echo around the whole house, juddering the windows. Honey and Danya took a step back and waited.

Thank goodness, Honey thought, almost relieved there was no answer.

'Shall I—?' Danya began.

'Absolutely not! You heard that knock echo around the whole house. There's clearly no one home . . . if in fact there's ever been anyone home since the war. Please, let's go to the fountain and wait for the others. I'm freaking out!' Honey pleaded.

Danya nodded and followed her sister to the garden. As Honey fought with the garden-gate padlock, Danya glanced back at the house just in time to see Peter, the postman, popping something through their letterbox. She ran over.

'Hi,' she said, slightly awkwardly.

'Hello,' Peter said, not quite sure what she wanted with him.

'Erm, I just wanted to . . . err, ask you about our neighbours at number forty-five. I live at forty-four you see and we . . . that is, our other neighbours at number seven are . . . erm . . . having a party on Friday night and wanted to give errr . . .'

She paused to scramble around in her bag and pulled out the invitation Maria had given her for her parents . . . *perfect*!

'Errrrr . . . this party invitation through the door. The problem is we don't have a name to put on it and Mum says there's nothing more rude than sending an invitation without a name on it,' Danya said, scarcely believing the tales that were coming out of her own mouth.

'I'm sorry, I don't . . . ?' Peter looked confused, not least because on the rare occasions he'd had to meet the occupant of forty-five Beaufort Square in the past twenty or so years, he never met anyone less likely to attend a party.

'I guess I'm asking if you know the owner of number forty-five's name? So we can invite them?' Danya said quickly, legs, arms and fingers all crossed.

Peter weighed it up. What harm could it do to give someone's name? Heck, he'd even write it on himself and post it through the door.

'Let's see now. She doesn't get much post these days but I think you mean Miss Page . . .' He rummaged around in his trolley. 'Ah, yes, I thought so, there's a letter for her today actually. It's addressed to Miss Lizzie Page. I tell you what . . . why don't you give yours to me and I'll see she gets it.'

And before she could say another word Danya watched, open-mouthed as Postman Peter took a pen from behind his ear, scrawled *Miss Lizzie Page* in one corner of the invitation and popped it through the letterbox at number forty-five along with the other letter.

Oooops, Danya thought. Oh well. The plan was to get a name and it worked.

'HONEY! Wait up!'

And she ran to join the others.

'Page . . .' Molly said slowly on the phone to Maria. 'P-A-G-E. Miss Lizzie Page. Can you believe it, Mimi! We have a name!'

'Well done, girls,' Maria said. 'Danya, can you hear me?'

'Yes, you're on speaker. I can hear you,' Danya said.

'Great job. As luck would have it, I'm not leaving the office at all today as LT's been called home on family business. She's left me some research, but nothing I can't do quickly so I'll have plenty of time in the archives to do some digging about our Miss Page.'

'Fantastic. And we'll tackle the church to see if we can find a tunnel!' Molly said, grabbing the phone from Danya before she could respond.

'Excellent. Over. Love you. Over!' Molly shouted.

'Molly, you're not on the walkie-talkie now!' Maria giggled.

'Yes, sorry! It's just I'm all missioned up and ready for action,' Molly said, smoothing her hair behind her ears.

'Come on then, let's go, agent F2,' Pippa said, remembering their code names from past adventures.

'Hey, I want a name!' Honey said, as they hung up.

'Agent S2, fall in line. We've got work to do!' Pippa announced and started walking in the direction of the Sacred Heart Church.

Honey grinned. Agent S2 wasn't particularly glamorous but it would do for now.

'This is ridiculous. There's no sign of a grille or anything. Got any Mrs Dundas treats in that rucksack, Agent Burrows?' Honey said, praying for something sweet.

'Sure have, Agent Sawyer,' Pippa said.

'Ahhhhh!' Honey said, chomping on a deliciously sugary flapjack.

'We've combed every inch of this cemetery and church garden but there's no sign of a grass-covered, overgrown, bramble-strewn tunnel entrance anywhere. It's hopeless!' Sally moaned.

'I've got closer to more tombstones and touched more graves than I care to think about this morning,' Honey said. 'I think maybe we got this one wrong. I don't think there is a secret entrance here after all.'

Danya jumped up suddenly, her eyes twinkling.

'I've got an idea!' she said and walked over to the north end of the church wall.

'What if you're right? What if the entrance isn't secret?' she whispered. 'What if it's in plain view of everyone and has been all this time?'

'I don't believe it. You think that little door in the side of the church is the tunnel entrance?' Pippa said.

'Sure, why not? Anyone would just think it leads into the church. Come to think of it, the tunnel did look like it was blocked with wooden slats rather than a board when we looked last night, which would work with the panelling on the door. What do you say, agents? Shall we go for it?'

Pippa scanned the area around for any nosy onlookers. 'Clear! Go for it,' she said.

Danya lifted the latch, which was stiff with rust but immediately the door moved and they were able to tug it open. And lo and behold, on the other side was a grille and behind it a set of steep steps led down into a dark, gloomy tunnel.

'We've found it!' Honey said, ecstatic.

'Yes, but we can't get in, can we? We're so stupid! Why didn't we think to loosen the grille from the inside last night?' Danya groaned.

Molly launched forwards, rummaging in her pockets.

'Molly . . . what are you . . . ?' Sally cried.

But it was too late. Molly had puffed out a whole tube of glitter down into the tunnel. The whole place was glistening.

'Molly! Have you completely lost your mind? What were you thinking?' Danya said as the rest of the gang got the complete giggles.

Molly looked distraught. 'I was just trying to be a bit clever like you marked up our tunnels with chalk. I couldn't find any chalk in the craft box, but thought this glitter would work just as well, if not better in torchlight.'

'But, Molly . . . we already knew which tunnel it was . . . it's the only one with the steps . . . remember?'

'Oh, right. Yes,' Molly said, mortified. 'Please don't tell, Mimi. I.N.L.I.D!'

(INLID = I'll never live it down, Story-seeker)

The others didn't know how they were going to keep this one secret. It was too funny not to share.

'Personally I can't wait to see the fairy tunnel by torchlight from the other side,' Honey said, giving Molly's hand a squeeze. 'Come on girls, let's get that grille off!'

By the time the girls reached number seven Beaufort Square, they'd had a text from Maria to say she'd had no luck with the name Lizzie Page, which had sent them all into a bit of a tail spin. She'd even tried every variation of Lizzie – Elizabeth, Liz, Elspeth – but nothing had thrown up anything remotely connected with Mina Ballerina.

Despite their incredible discovery of the bomb shelter, the original mystery of the missing ballerina was as much of a mystery now as ever.

'Well, if we know nothing else about poor Mina Ballerina, at least we're almost certain about how she escaped, or was taken . . . even if we don't know why or by whom!' Danya said as the girls approached the newly named 'fairy tunnel' from inside the shelter.

'It's just not enough though,' Pippa said. 'Her story deserves to be heard. It's not enough for someone's memory to be a mystery.'

'Look, don't lose heart. Maria's still on it. She might find something,' Molly said.

'I know, I just don't have a good feeling about it. The name Lizzie Page has nothing whatsoever to do with Mina Elizabeth King and we couldn't even find anything under that name,' Danya said.

'Perhaps it's time for Maria to take this to LT. Especially as the unpublished article she showed us was by a relative of hers. Do we know what the relationship is yet?' asked Danya.

'Maria did some research on Horatio and came up trumps there. What did she say about him the other night, Sally? Oh, that was it. Horatio was LT's father and one of the most famous journalists the *Gazette* had ever known. Nothing eluded him. Once he had the bit between his teeth with a story, he would dig and dig and dig until every last truth was uncovered,' Molly said.

'Not this time. Something stopped the great HT and hopefully LT might know what,' Pippa said.

'Well, that's up to Maria, but you know what she's like about sharing a story before it's finished. I shouldn't imagine she'll want to admit defeat so quickly, especially in front of LT,' Molly said. 'We'll have to work on her together tonight. It's her last day at the *Gazette* tomorrow so it's now or never. And I can't face a lifetime of not knowing what happened to that poor girl every time I look at her statue.'

'If you don't think Maria's going to ask LT for help, then it's back to plan A,' Danya said with conviction as she undid the last bolt on the Sacred Heart Church grille.

'I can't even remember what plan A was, but I don't like the sound of your tone, sis,' Honey said, knowing Danya meant business when her voice went all low like that.

'I think she's referring to "taking a peek at number forty-five",' Pippa said. 'And I have to say, this time, I think she might be right. Who knows what we might uncover in that cellar about the King family and what happened. If we're going to get some answers, it's the only place left to explore.'

Danya looked at Pippa, grateful for her support.

'Oh, I don't know,' Molly groaned, understandably worried about breaking into someone's home.

'Look, it's not like we're going to run around the whole house. We're just taking a little peek around their cellar. There's usually just a load of old junk and dust in a cellar. No harm done. I bet Miss Page hasn't been down there this century, let alone recently enough to catch us,' Sally said, also on Danya's side.

'Can we at least wait until Maria gets home tonight to see what she thinks? I wouldn't feel right until I have her thoughts on it,' Molly said, feeling peer pressure to agree.

'Of course! We can't do it without Maria anyway. She always spots something the rest of us don't,' Danya said.

'Let's just hope she doesn't spot my glitter handiwork while she's at it! She'll go ballistic!' Molly said.

Although she was secretly sure that even Maria would have to admit how beautiful the glittering cave of diamonds was in the torchlight.

10

Maria's Resolve to Shake Up the Situation

*M*aria had spent the morning researching a street artist called Banksy for LT. To this day, Banksy's true identity remains a total secret. There are no pictures of him and it's clear that anyone who does know who he is guards the secret with their lives. Every now and again one of his pictures appears on a wall or a building somewhere and hits the headlines. He is the perfect mystery, one which no one has yet managed to solve.

It made Maria think again of her own dead end, the one she'd hit that morning with her research into Miss Page. She'd hoped with every inch of her being that somehow that name would lead to a cascade of information she could use to solve the mystery.

As far as she could see, they had two options. Option one was to pretend none of it had ever happened and forget all about Mina and just be happy with their discovery of the bomb shelter. Or two, ask LT for help when she had only half a story, but that went against every principle she had. Not one for giving up, she decided to go with option two and risk disappointing her hero. She'd write up what she had, then ask LT for some time tomorrow morning, her last day at the *Gazette*, and see if she could throw any light on it. To be honest, the information she had on the missing ballerina wasn't much, but she hoped that the tunnel maze below Beaufort Square might jazz up the story enough to spark LT's interest. She also had the fact that it was LT's own father who'd originally chased the story and who'd shelved it for some unknown reason. Knowing LT as she did, if that fact didn't jog her into action, nothing would. It was worth a shot. Perhaps the Tangerella family kept a private archive somewhere with all the answers. Wishful thinking!

Her mind was made up and whatever happened with solving the mystery, at least sharing the story with LT would be the perfect way to thank her for all the opportunities she'd given her that week. So Maria tucked herself away in one of the corner offices and began to write their story.

'Maria. Oh there you are, dear!' LT said, making Maria jump out of her skin as she appeared at her desk.

'Hi! How was your day?' Maria said, quickly gathering up her notes. She'd totally lost track of time.

'Oh, marvellous, although not without drama,' LT said, casting her beady eye over Maria's papers. 'And you've had a good day too, it would seem.'

'Hmmm?' Maria said, looking guilty.

'The Banksy research. A thorough job, Maria, well done. But I've come to expect nothing less from you. I particularly loved the interview you found with the woman claiming to be his grandmother. Who knows, eh? Who knows?' LT mused.

'Right. Yes!' Maria. 'Fascinating story. I'd never heard of him before. Can't imagine anyone managing to keep him secret for so long. Someone, somewhere must eventually decide to tell.'

'Yes, one would think so. Anyway, off you pop. Last day tomorrow and I'm not sure where I'm sending you yet, but there'll be something come in overnight which you can get your teeth into,' she said, turning to leave.

'Actually,' Maria said. 'About tomorrow. I know it's a bit of a cheek but I wondered if you might have fifteen minutes or so in your diary to talk through something I've been working on.'

LT swung around, her eyebrows raised inquisitively. Suddenly she looked like an eagle, about to swoop on its prey.

'A story you've been working on, Maria?'

Maria nodded. 'Why, how intriguing. I'll be in at 9 a.m. sharp. If you can make it into my office before I do with a glass of freshly squeezed orange juice from the canteen, I'll be all ears until 9.30 a.m. Deal?'

'Deal!' Maria said joyfully. 'Fresh orange juice. Absolutely!' But LT had already left the room.

Oh my goodness, I'm going to be up all night finishing this article now. I hope the girls have got something juicy to add! she thought to herself.

But little did Maria know that the Beaufort Square supersleuths had other plans for her that evening.

11

The Beaufort Six go A-Snooping

'Maria! Where have you been?' Molly called down the stairs in desperation when she heard the door.

'I'm sorry! I didn't notice the time,' Maria started but was prevented from going upstairs to see the girls by a fairly furious Linda Fitzfoster bursting through the sitting-room door.

'Maria, do you know it's nearly eight o'clock? It's far too late for you to be walking through the front door! I might call Miss Tangerella and give her a piece of my mind. What does she think this is? Slave labour?'

'Mum, no! Don't, please don't! LT . . . I mean Miss Tangerella wasn't even in the office this afternoon. I was working on something for school and completely lost track of time,' Maria pleaded as her dad entered the hall.

'Darling, she's home now and that's what counts,' Brian said gently to his wife, in an attempt to calm her. 'And she'll make sure she's home by 3 p.m. tomorrow – in good time for the party – right, Maria?'

'Right, yes Dad. Absolutely!' Maria promised, hoping it was a promise she'd be able to keep.

'Now get yourself down to the kitchen for Mrs D's toad-in-the-hole supper. She's saved you some in the oven – although you're lucky it's lasted this long with those vulture friends of yours,' he continued as giggles floated down from the top floor.

'Thanks, Dad. Sorry, Mum. It really was my fault. I've only got one more day at the Gazette and I don't want to waste a second of it. I really have learned a mountain about the press industry,' and Maria as she bounded down to the kitchen, the thought of crispy Yorkshire pudding, sausage and gravy overwhelming her. She hadn't eaten all day and, boy, was she hungry!

♡ ♥ ♡

By the time Maria had finished with supper and another quick chat with her parents, it was nine o'clock. Most definitely time for bed, as she'd been reliably informed by her mother.

Opening the bedroom door and seeing the light off, she crept across to her bed and flicked on the little night-light on her bedside table. Silently, she lifted the pillow, looking for her pyjamas and notebook so she could jot down anything extra she thought of for her presentation to LT in the morning.

She glanced over to Molly, who was gently purring in her sleep. Then noticed a head pointing out of the other end of Molly's duvet. A head of thick, dark hair. *Pippa!* She thought. What was she doing in . . .

'Surprise!' Sally said, jumping out of the wardrobe in her long pink fluffy dressing gown.

'What are you playing at, you lot?' Maria whispered angrily. 'Sally, you scared me half to death! And as for you, sister dear, first you're desperate to see me as soon as I walk through the front door – then I come upstairs and you're all asleep! What's going on?'

'Get dressed and you'll find out!' Pippa squealed from under Molly's duvet.

'Get dressed? What do you mean, get dressed?!'

Maria said, feeling more tired and more irritable by the second.

'Tah-dah!' Sally said, throwing off her robe.

'Tah-dah!' Molly and Pippa said in unison as they threw back their duvet.

A large smile crossed Maria's face as she looked at the girls' black assassin outfits.

It was always a good night when the black leggings came out. It's just that usually Maria was in charge of the whole operation. Not this time though, Story-seeker. For the first time ever, she was completely in the dark – and we're not just talking about the colour of her outfit.

'Tell me everything! NOW!' she demanded.

Maria had to admit she was a little bit hesitant, if not a bit disappointed. With the build-up the girls had given, she'd at least thought they'd found another clue about Mina Ballerina. She had to admit they'd done really well finding the fairy tunnel – although goodness only knows why they'd given it that stupid name!

She'd see, Story-seeker, she'd see! HA!

But was this really the plan now? To break in and snoop around someone's basement and hope for a miracle? Oh well, they'd solved mysteries on less.

'Come on then, agents. Let's do this!' And with that, four black-clad assassins crept down to the Fitzfoster cellar, careful to skip every creaky floorboard on the way.

'What about D and H?' Maria asked.

'I radioed them before we left the bedroom. They'll meet us under the fountain,' Pippa said.

'Excellent! And I see you have my trusty rucksack, Pips. I have taught you well. Torches?'

'Check,' Pippa whispered back.

'Screwdrivers – Philips and flat head?' Maria asked.

'Check, check,' Pippa said.

'Hammer?' Maria asked.

'Will you shut up, Mimi! Honestly, how do you think we've coped without you this past week!' Molly snapped. 'Now let's go. The others will be waiting!'

'The mind boggles!' Maria said under her breath, seeing how much her little apprentices had come on this past week.

'I was just thinking . . .' Maria said as the tunnel opened up into the main shelter.

Molly rolled her eyes. *Why couldn't Maria just trust her for once!*

'I'll ignore that . . .' Maria continued, impressed with how much less stressed out she was feeling in the tunnel this time round. 'I was just thinking, what happens if forty-five's cellar is boarded up from the inside like ours was?'

'It's not,' came a familiar voice from the shadows.

'Danya! Honey!' Maria said, happy to see them, but trying not to laugh at their assassin gear. Honey had gone one step further and put on a dark bob wig and black stripes across each cheek. *What was she like?*

'We checked that when we were looking for the tunnel out to street level, remember?' Pippa said. 'It's definitely accessible from the tunnel. Unless we can't shift whatever's propped up behind it, but there's no way of knowing that until we get the grille off.'

'Sorry – yes, you did say that. I feel a bit out of the loop having not been here all that much. I shan't say another word. You've obviously got this covered. Lead the way, agents,' Maria said and the six midnight detectives took the tunnel next to the Sawyers'.

Somehow the whole experience of being in the old tunnel network felt creepier than ever. Perhaps it had something to do with it being night time. Perhaps it had something to do with the sorts of noises you might expect to hear underground in the dark, insects and larger animals scurrying and scratching about, water dripping. Even the smell seemed more pungent and the air heavier. Perhaps it was just the fact that the six friends were about to enter the unknown, and illegally at that.

 The risks certainly seemed to be outweighing the results, Story-seeker. Let's hope that changed soon.

Finally, they reached the end of the tunnel where they found it just as Sally and Pippa had described. Danya and Pippa got to work on the bolts, which undid surprisingly easily given their rusty appearance.

It took just under ten minutes to loosen the grille completely and lay it down on the floor.

'Right! And now the moment of truth!' Danya said. 'Push!' she called as six pairs of hands got to work.

'Oh for goodness' sake!' Molly whispered. 'Nothing's ever simple is it? Whatever this is that's blocking it, it might as well be screwed to the wall! We don't want whatever it is to topple over. That would literally be the end for us!'

It moved, shifting forwards just enough for them to be able to squeeze around it.

'It's a piano!' Honey said.

'A-choo!' Sally tried to muffle a sneeze.

'SSSSHHHHH!' the others panicked.

'Sorry! I'm not great with dust!' Sally answered.

'Now she tells us!' Pippa giggled.

'But the tunnels are full of dust and you haven't been sneezing there.'

'Perhaps it's just breaking and entering dust that affects me then – I don't know!' Sally grinned.

'Hey! Have you forgotten what we're here for?' Danya said, trying to bring some order back to the group. 'Let's just shine our lights and assess what we're dealing with first, before we start rummaging about.'

'Good idea,' Honey said.

'Ready?' Danya asked when they were all either side of the heaviest piano in the world which had blocked the entrance to the tunnel.

'Torches on!' Maria said.

GASP! was followed by a muffled squeal from one of the terrified girls – then the torches were quickly switched off. Facing them in the dark were six people, armed with flashlights and seemingly ready to attack.

As Molly started to make a run for it, Honey grabbed her arm. 'Molly, it's OK. I . . . I think . . . it's a mirror!' Honey said.

'A mirror?' Molly said, switching her torch back on. 'Yes! Clever Honey – it's just our reflection! Girls! It's just a mirror.'

'For a moment there I thought we were truly goners!' Molly whispered to Honey.

As their torches scanned the cellar before them, they soon saw that it had floor-to-ceiling mirrors on all the walls, with a rail running horizontally along the middle of the room.

'It's . . . a dance studio!' Honey whispered, immediately reminded of the Bolshoi rooms at L'Etoile.

On the far side was a table with an old gramophone and a pile of vinyl records, still in their sleeves. To their right was an enormous ornate wardrobe, housing a pile of dancing shoes and some outfits hanging in moth-eaten dust bags. On the far left wall there were a couple of trunks and a large bureau. Essentially though, apart from the aforementioned objects, it was just a huge empty space.

'Something tells me this isn't your average cellar full of junk!' Danya said.

'One thing we do know is that nothing's been touched down here for years. Look how thick the dust is everywhere,' Honey said.

'Which gives us a whole different set of problems. The problem with untouched dust is that it might as well be a fresh layer of snow. As soon as we get our paws on anything, there'll be visible evidence of us being here,' Maria said.

'Well, we can't investigate without rummaging in a few boxes,' Danya said, desperate to go through absolutely everything.

'And I just love those old gramophones,' Pippa said. 'Uncle Harry has a picture of one with a dog next to it in his studio. He said it inspired a generation. I'd love to see one up close.'

'I just might be one step ahead of you little lot!' Sally said suddenly, her eyes flashing with cunning.

Ever since, Danya's brainwave with the chalk, Molly's not-so-brainwave with the glitter and Maria's . . . well, brainwave after brainwave, she'd been trying to think of something she could contribute. The idea had come to her when she was scrabbling around under her bed for her old black leggings and noticed the mess she'd made on the dusty floorboards as she searched. It had occurred to her then that the cellar at number forty-five might be dusty, so how would they cover their tracks?

'I just happen to have a solution for this very problem,' she announced proudly, pulling out a large bag of wholemeal flour and three large sieves.

'Sally, you'd best tell us now if you're planning on baking a cake this evening as it's neither the time, nor the place!' Molly giggled.

'Noooo! Don't you get it? Once we've finished looking through something we shouldn't, we sieve flour over the top to replace the dust we've disturbed. It's not perfect but it's a start.'

The others just stared at her in disbelief.

 Sometimes, Story-seeker, practical genius came from the most surprising of places!

Pippa leaned over and gave her the biggest kiss on the cheek. 'My twin, you are brilliant!'

'Yes, bravo, Sal!' Danya said.

'What forethought!' Maria said. 'Not sure that would have occurred to me in a million years!'

Sally was pleased they couldn't see her blushes and thrilled to have finally reached genius status.

'I chose the wholemeal flour as it's not such a stark colour as white flour. Don't want it to end up looking like it's snowed in here, do we?' she added.

'If it was up to me, I'd replace the dust with glitter,' Molly giggled as she shot the others a knowing glance.

'Well thank goodness it's not up to you, you crazy cat!' Maria said. She couldn't think of anything more inappropriate, covering all this history with a layer of fairy dust.

Wink, wink, Story-seeker!

'Right agents, let's get to work, and remember, we're looking for anything out of the ordinary which might shed light on Mina's disappearance,' Danya said, spotting the longing in Honey's eyes to try on a tutu she'd just found in the wardrobe.

Excitement pulsated through the room, each girl positive she was going to find the one thing that would crack the case wide open.

Danya was on her second shoebox before she announced she'd found a contract between the Sadler's Wells Ballet company and Mina Elizabeth King to join their first national tour.

'Oh my, we're getting close now! I can feel it!' she whispered to herself as she took some photos of the documents and grabbed a sieve before replacing them exactly as they were.

Then Maria opened one of the bureau drawers to reveal several hanging files and in one of the compartments, she found the last will and testament of Mr Charles King. As she read, she gasped. *Elizabeth Page!* There was her name as clear as the ink it was written in. She read out loud for the others to hear.

'Agents! Over here! Listen up! It's Mina's father's will! . . . *I ,Charles Andrew King, in the event of my death and the absence of any known and present surviving family, do bequeath my estate to my faithful housekeeper, Miss Elizabeth Page . . .* '

'Oh my gosh. Lizzie Page was the housekeeper! And she's still alive and living upstairs!' Molly said.

'She must know everything. We need to see her, Maria!' Danya said.

'Let's keep looking. We've done really well so far. If we find enough evidence, then we can see if LT will pay her a visit and get her to talk,' Maria said, feeling more confident by the second. In less than an hour in that cellar they'd found out more than in a whole week's worth of trawling the internet and *Gazette* archives. She took photos of the will and replaced it in the file, careful to sieve a little flour over her prints.

'One thing that the will and Elizabeth Page living upstairs proves is that Mina Ballerina is definitely deceased, or she surely would have come to claim her inheritance,' Honey said, thoughtfully.

'Unless she couldn't! Unless she was being held prisoner somewhere. What if Elizabeth Page is the bad one in all this and had Mina locked up somewhere so she could steal the King family fortune for herself?' Molly said.

'No theory can be discounted at this stage,' Maria said. 'Anything's possible until we know for sure.'

After the excitement of finding the will, Sally and Pippa returned to admiring the beautiful gramophone. Both of them longed to hear it play some of the records that were there. All appeared to be classical pieces – none of which Sally had heard of and she should know. Her mum, Maggie, had been obsessed with classical music and virtually fed Sally on it from birth. But these records all had foreign names – some German, some French, some in languages she didn't even recognise. She thought perhaps she might recognise the song titles if she knew the English translation, but even her German was too basic for that. It struck her as slightly odd that the record on the gramophone was clean as a whistle, whilst the rest of the place was such a dust pit, but was distracted by trying to make out the song title.

Pippa pulled another box from under the gramophone table. Lifting the lid, she saw dozens and dozens more records. She thought how much Uncle Harry would love to see them. He was always harping on about how digitally recorded music just didn't sound the same as vinyl. Suddenly she noticed a piece of string sticking up through one of the floorboards and as she pulled it, one of the boards lifted to reveal a little package wrapped in a hessian type of material. *How* curious, she thought, wondering what she might have stumbled on. As she tugged at the string, the fabric fell away to reveal a beautifully painted miniature Russian doll, the sort which is a doll within a doll. Suddenly she was distracted by Molly calling them all over to the staircase in a panic.

'Did anyone move these from the wardrobe and forget to put them back?' Molly said, holding up an immaculate pair of pale pink ballet shoes.

Everyone shook their heads.

'I hate to say it but these don't look old and dusty to me. In fact, they're brand new and the same make mine are. I think we might have been a bit hasty in concluding that no one ever comes down here!' Molly said again, her heart beginning to beat harder in her chest.

'Let me see those shoes,' Honey said, running her fingertips along the bottom then smelling them. 'Fresh rosin!' she said.

'What?' the others answered.

'Rosin, or powdered rosin, to be precise. Dancers quite often put rosin powder on the bottom of their shoes to stop them from slipping on slippy floors,' Honey continued.

'And you reckon someone's been down here with the rosin, recently?' Sally said, suddenly all ears.

'An educated guess? Yes!' Honey said.

'But I thought we checked! I thought you said there was dust everywhere, and I quote "no one's been down here for years!'" Molly said to Maria.

'We all looked and agreed!' Maria whispered back.

'I don't remember checking the floor. There could have been a million footprints on the floor that I don't remember checking. I was only looking around the room on the tables and boxes and stuff,' Danya admitted.

Maria nodded. *She could be right*, she thought.

'Then what are we still doing here? Let's dust over and get out!' Molly said. 'Lizzie Page might have a young relative or friend staying with her who's using the studio. We've got to leave it as we found it, or they'll know someone's been in here!'

And within ninety seconds, the girls had floured the room, pulled back the piano, and replaced the grille to number forty-five's cellar.

'Is everybody all right?' Honey whispered to the others as they lay panting on the tunnel floor, waiting for their hearts to stop thumping.

'That was close!' Sally said. 'But then, I no longer know what it feels like not to get through a situation by the skin of our teeth!'

The girls all began to laugh.

'Oh Sal! You have such a way with words,' Pippa said. 'Come on, let's go to bed. We can get up early and run through all the photos in the morning before your meeting with LT, Maria.'

'Night, twins!' Sally called out as the Sawyers took their tunnel.

'Night, quads!' Honey shouted back.

And with that, six exhausted little adventurers tumbled into bed unable to believe they'd come through another adventure unscathed!

12

A Consultation with the Tangerella Family

Not surprisingly, Maria slept right through her seven o'clock alarm, waking at five minutes to eight, which barely gave her enough time for a shower if she was to be ready and waiting in LT's office by nine sharp.

'Molly,' she said, plucking the ear-plug out of her sleeping sister's ear as she was about to leave.

'Hmmmm?' Molly groaned.

'Moll! Wake up, it's important,' Maria said.

'Are the ballet shoes coming?' Molly mumbled in her sleep.

'Ballet shoes? No! What are you on about? Wake

up, Moll!' Maria said, shaking her a bit harder.

'Maria? What is it? Is she coming?' Molly sat bolt upright.

'I've no idea what you're talking about, but listen, I've overslept and not had time to gather together all the photos we took last night. Can you wake the others up and go through everything? Email me anything we haven't already noted that you think might be important. I'm sure we missed something among all the paperwork last night,' Maria said, nervous as anything about her presentation to LT.

'Sure, Mimi! Will do it now. Good luck this morning. You're a natural born reporter and don't you forget it. LT will be eating out of your hand by the time you've finished!' Molly said and gave her sister a hug goodbye.

'Right then, here goes nothing!' she whispered and ran down to where the ever-obliging Eddie was ready and waiting in the car outside with a welcome cup of steaming hot chocolate.

Maria's eyes never left the clock in LT's office. One minute to nine. *Thank goodness she'd made it – yet*

again – by the skin of her teeth. In fact – had she even cleaned her teeth this morning? Who cares, too late now. What mattered was that she had the fresh orange and she wasn't late!

'Good morning, Maria,' LT boomed as she swooshed over to her desk. And before she'd even finished hanging her coat up, she launched into action.

'Now tell me, Miss Fitzfoster, what could you possibly want with one of my father's old unpublished articles about a missing ballerina?'

Maria's jaw hit the floor. This woman was a witch! She had to be.

'How did you kno—?'

'Know? How did I know?' LT said, sitting back in her chair and taking a large sip of juice. 'Why, Maria, dear, I didn't get the reputation for being the country's hottest investigative journalist by sitting back and waiting for the story to come to me.'

Maria was speechless. She couldn't work out whether LT was furious or happy so thought she'd better keep quiet until she did.

'I knew you were hot on the heels of something, Maria, so I looked into your archive research and voila! Your search history showed me exactly what you've been looking into. I hit every wall you hit, until

I remembered seeing the printout of an unpublished article on your desk last night – recognisable by the red stamp, obviously – so I hit that archive and discovered your interest in an article my father wrote in 1944.'

She fell silent. Maria got it. It was her turn to talk.

'You're absolutely right, of course. That's what I wanted to talk to you about this morning – and so much more . . .'

'More?' LT's eyes sparkled. 'How wonderful. I'm drenched in anticipation, Maria . . .'

And with that the whole story came tumbling out, starting with how the girls had discovered the missing date on the ballerina fountain; how they had found out that the date was wrong; discovered the underground tunnel system and bomb shelter under Beaufort Square; the escape route through the Sacred Heart Church; and, thanks to Horatio Tangerella's unpublished article, that Mina Ballerina had lived at number forty-five. And that the old housekeeper, Miss Page, was the sole occupant now, having been left everything in Mr King's will, which, Maria added, proved that his daughter and wife must be dead. She, of course, kept to herself the fact that the girls had entered the cellar at number forty-five in the dead of night, completely illegally.

By the time Maria stopped talking, both she and LT were flushed. What a story. It had everything: a rise to fame, heartbreak, a dark family secret, a secret passage and to top it all the mystery surrounding why the story of the missing ballerina had never been published.

'I have no idea why my father would have sat on such a story,' LT said at last, after she'd digested everything. 'But I'm hoping he might be able to tell us himself,' she went on.

Maria looked like she might be about to see another ghost. She knew for a fact that Horatio Tangerella had died in 1990 as she'd seen his obituary during her research. Seeing Maria turn pale, LT jumped up.

'Oh Maria, no dear, I don't mean in person. Of course, my dear father is no longer with us but I'm hoping he may tell us something by way of us going through his old files,' LT continued.

Maria's eyes followed LT as she pulled some files from her briefcase. They were bound in red leather with matching ties, which she loosened before placing on the coffee table.

'My father kept a mini archive at the house

which backed up all of his reporting at the *Gazette*. Sometimes I find that the files are exactly the same as the *Gazette* archive, but every now and again I find extra notes there, which he didn't want to leave in public hands. It's a tradition I've upheld, and something which you would do well to copy yourself. You never know when someone might need a helping hand in the future!'

'This is more than I could have hoped for!' Maria exclaimed.

'Don't count your chickens yet. It's nearly killed me to do so but, as this is your story, Maria, I've stopped myself from going through them without you. I just hope Father has left some answers for us. There are two files here encompassing 1944. You take one and I'll take the other and whoever finds anything exciting makes the tea!'

'Deal!' Maria said, thinking about anything other than tea.

Her heart was pounding as she untied the red leather strap on her file. Suddenly about a hundred papers scattered to the floor. It was all loose!

'I'm so sorry!' she said, red-faced as she started to scoop them up. 'It never occurred to me that the pages wouldn't be bound inside.'

'Ha! Don't worry. I made exactly the same mistake the first time I opened one. I should have remembered to tell you. My father wasn't known for his organisation,' LT said, draining her orange juice.

'Gosh, the dates will be all over the place now,' Maria said, furious she might have cost herself valuable discovery time.

She knelt on the floor, scanning every scrap of paper but saw nothing about Mina Ballerina. As she got to the last sheet of paper, her disappointment was painful. Nothing. Absolutely nothing. She didn't say anything to LT until she saw her close her own file and tie it back up.

'Oh, Maria. I'm sorry for having raised your hopes like this. The reasons for Father not publishing that article are so mysterious, I felt sure he would have explained himself here,' LT said.

Maria was devastated. Not half an hour ago LT's office had been pulsating with promise and excitement; now they were back to square one and none the wiser. She tied up her file and walked over to the desk.

'Maria, we can still do a piece on the Beaufort bomb shelter. Let's not forget that discovery . . . WAIT!'

LT said, suddenly pointing to where Maria had been sitting. 'You've missed a bit.'

Maria walked back over to a crumpled, bottom-squashed note, lying face down on the fluffy rug. WATC this is it? she thought to herself.

As she picked it up and turned it over, her face lit up with happiness.

'Well . . . do share, Maria, dear,' LT said.

Maria read out loud:

<u>Case of missing ballerina – Mina Elizabeth King</u>
<u>– SHELVED – HIGH RISK</u>

Mysterious disappearance before the performance, which would launch her into classical dance stratosphere. Friend of mine, Henry Biggins from the theatre, contacted me with initial info so went straight to King residence at 45 Beaufort Square, London to interview father, Charles King. Charles King saw me straight away. Took great risk in sharing his story with me – and for that I rewarded his honesty with my silence. Mina Elizabeth was born to Russian parents in Moscow where they lived until the death of her mother when Mina was five years old. Charles also revealed that he had been working for the British

Intelligence Services as well as for Russia. In short, he was a double agent. Devastated at the loss of his wife and worried about the safety of his young daughter and himself too, he moved to London under an assumed identity. Charles King is not his real name. Mina was raised as English. Following in the footsteps of her mother, who had been a member of the Bolshoi Ballet, she showed great promise in ballet and trained hard, earning a place at the academy and then the tour which was to launch her career, but pride and excitement turned to anger when her father seemed unwilling for her to take her place in the limelight. Of course, he was worried that somehow, after years of safety, they might somehow be recognised. After a furious argument with her father Mina disappeared and was never seen again. Charles King revealed these truths to me and begged me not to publish the story to protect his only daughter. Even with his spy links, he couldn't trace Mina and the worst of it was he couldn't be sure whether she had run away of her own accord through anger, or whether she had been kidnapped by Russian spies as a punishment for his defection. Whatever happened to Mina, printing their story would only put her *at risk. I agreed without hesitation and helped to squash other press interest. I am an honourable man and only write for the greater good. In this case, the safety of Mina Elizabeth King, wherever she may be, was the greater good. Case closed.*

'Wow!' Maria gasped, everything suddenly becoming clear. 'Whatever happened to her, Mina must have used the tunnels under Beaufort Square to make her escape or worse. It would have been the only way no one saw her go.'

'Indeed. What a tragic story you've uncovered, Maria,' LT said.

'But it's so sad. He was trying to protect his daughter, but he couldn't tell her the truth and it drove her away from him and her home; it's as though she died anyway. He didn't even know what date to put on her memorial statue in the square. I can't bear it,' Maria said tearfully.

'What do you think we should do with this information now, Maria? Should we tell Mina's story – as far as we have been able to follow it? We have a pretty good idea of how she might have escaped and can use photos, the old photos from my father's article of Mina and her father, and take new shots of the memorial fountain and her route through the tunnels,' LT said, piecing together the article in her mind. 'I know it's Friday already, but if we get our skates on, we could go to print over the weekend for a special piece next week. Happy?'

'Over the moon. Thank you so much for helping me piece all this together,' Maria said, desperate to phone the girls and fill them in.

'There are just a few things I'd like to check first. I'd love to see the tunnels and I think we ought to try to interview the housekeeper . . .' LT paused to glance at her notes. 'Miss . . .'

'Page, Miss Elizabeth Page. We tried knocking on her door but there wasn't any answer. None of us have ever seen her,' Maria said.

'Perhaps we'll have more luck if we go together. I just wouldn't feel as though we'd exhausted every avenue until we've at least tried to talk to her,' LT said.

'We thought that too, but I don't think she'll even answer the door,' said Maria.

'Sometimes, Maria dear, when a secret has been buried for as long as this one has, the truth is desperate to get out. The holder is just waiting for the opportunity to feel that they are not betraying a trust. It's just a question of how you ask. I think if we make

Miss Page feel like she owes it to Mina and the world to share what she knows, she just might talk.'

Maria wasn't so sure, but she had every faith that if anyone could make her talk, it was the silver-tongued Luscious Tangerella!

And with that, Maria and LT left the *Gazette* offices with identical swooshes.

13

Luscious Tangerella comes
to Beaufort Square

It was almost midday by the time the *Gazette* limo
pulled up outside number seven Beaufort Square.
LT and Maria had discussed how it might be sensible
to run through the whole story with Linda Fitzfoster
before taking it any further, seeing as both her home
and daughters would play a large part in its exposure.

While LT sat with Linda in their sitting room,
Maria had run upstairs to catch up on the morning's
events with the others.

'Oh the poor girl!' Molly said.

'Imagine that, having your hopes and dreams dashed
like that and not even knowing why,' Sally said.

'How tragic that such a super talent went to waste,' Honey said.

'I don't want to even think about her being kidnapped. Perhaps she just went back to Russia, back to her mother's roots, if she was so angry with her father,' Pippa said, picturing the treasured Russian doll toy she'd found hidden in Mina's cellar.

'Well at the very least people will hear some of her story now. They'll read about her talent and her suffering,' Maria said. 'Anyway, I'd best get downstairs and see if Mum needs peeling off the ceiling yet. I'm sure she's blown several gaskets by now after hearing what we've all been up to – although thinking about it, it'll mainly be you lot in trouble. I've been in the office all week!'

'Why Maria, you—' Molly shouted after her, but Maria was already halfway down the stairs.

'Are you angry?' asked Maria gingerly as she peered around the sitting-room door.

'To be honest, darling, I don't know what to think. It's hopeless me scolding you girls as you seem to find adventure wherever you go. Honestly, I think you'd find a secret passage in a cardboard box! I'm more concerned that you only ever share your findings with an adult when it's absolutely necessary,' Linda Fitzfoster said, shaking her head in disbelief.

The others followed Maria into the room.

'Still, I must say, you've uncovered an extremely touching story this time and agree that perhaps Mina Ballerina's tale deserves to be told, so I've agreed with Miss Tangerella that she and her photographer may have access to our cellar and you girls for one hour this afternoon before the party,' Linda Fitzfoster continued. 'I just hope that your dad is in agreement. Luckily for you all, he's unobtainable for the next few hours so I've made the decision and will tell him later.'

'Oh Mum!' Maria rushed forwards, followed by five other grateful girls. 'You're the bestest! I promise, once this is over, we'll spend the rest of the afternoon perfecting our hats!'

'Sure you will!' Linda Fitzfoster raised a doubtful eyebrow.

'A pleasure to meet you again, Miss Tangerella. And thank you for the time you have given Maria this week. I honestly think if she could leave L'Etoile now to come and work for you at the *Gazette*, she'd do it in a heartbeat. The girls will show you everything you need to see. I have some last-minute party preparations to attend to so if you'll excuse me . . .'

'Of course. Thank you so much for your understanding, Mrs Fitzfoster. Maria shows real promise and is most definitely on my radar as one to watch!'

Linda Fitzfoster flashed an approving smile at LT and then left the room, but not before she'd also flashed Maria a disapproving frown at what she'd just been told.

'Oh, LT. Thanks so much for putting Mum in the picture. She'd have locked us princesses in the tower for the rest of the holidays I reckon! Where do you want to begin?' Maria said.

'What say we enter the tunnels from your cellar and you can bring me out onto the square via the church exit,' LT said.

'NO!' Molly said in alarm, remembering Maria hadn't yet seen her glittering fairy tunnel.

'Molly, don't be silly – that's perfect. That way the Sawyers won't need to be bothered at all and then we can go straight to number forty-five to see if we can get an interview with the housekeeper,' Maria said, confused by Molly's reaction.

'Okay . . . well, don't say I didn't warn you,' Molly said, suddenly seeing the funny side.

Honey's and Danya's shoulders were shaking with smothered giggles.

'I'm bringing the video for this one,' Sally said, wanting to record the action. 'Pippa and I will wait at the church entrance so we can capture you as you hit the fairy . . . I mean ve-ry lovely Sacred Heart tunnel,' Sally said.

Maria knew she was being set up for something but didn't have time to figure it out. And within seconds the Sawyers and the Fitzfosters were giving LT the finest tour Beaufort Square had to offer.

And up to a certain point, no one above ground would have been any the wiser, except for the explosive sound of Maria discovering Molly's redecoration of one of the most exciting finds of twenty-first-century London.

'MO-LLLLLLY!'

'I think we should leave this part to the professionals,' Danya said to Maria, as they stood in front of number forty-five. 'It might be a bit much all of us pitching up, particularly if Miss Page isn't used to visitors.'

'Thanks, Dan. Probably best if you guys head back to ours and see if Mum needs any help too. Anything to keep her on side at this stage!' Maria said, aware that her mum could still pull the plug on the girls' involvement with the story at any moment.

'Leave it with me!' Danya said with a wink.

'What's happening?' Molly said, having caught up from the fairy tunnel.

'You! What were you thinking?' Maria said, still horrified that her twin sister had chosen pixie dust to redecorate the bomb shelter with.

'Actually, I think it was rather an ingenious idea,' LT said. 'Brings a certain playfulness to your discovery. You are young girls after all, making use of the tools you had available to you. I wouldn't worry too much, Maria. Besides, it did look rather magical in the torchlight.'

'See!' Molly said, grinning like a Cheshire cat, and then disappeared off with the others before Maria could say another word.

Only Molly Fitzfoster, Story-seeker, could turn the ridiculous into an act of genius and silence the great Maria Fitzfoster.

14

Encounter with a Stranger

*K*nock, knock ...
Once again the knocking echoed throughout number forty-five Beaufort Square; even the windowpanes trembled with emptiness.

Maria and LT waited patiently on the top step, the sunshine warm on their backs.

'Wait a second. I can hear music playing. Can you hear it? It's coming from downstairs,' Maria said, wondering if it was the old gramophone (not that she could tell LT about that).

'I'll knock again,' LT said and within seconds, the music had stopped and they heard slow, steady footsteps in the hallway.

The door opened a few inches and half an old face appeared.

'Yes?'

'Miss Page, I'm so sorry to bother you,' LT began, speaking very quickly. 'I'm Luscious Tangerella, from the Gazette. I wonder if we might have a few minutes of your time to talk about the history of the—'

Slam!

'. . . square.' LT trailed off.

Maria looked at LT in dismay. She'd felt sure the great Tangerella would be welcomed in. She was, of course, forgetting that most people considered journalists to be nosy busy-bodies!

LT looked a little ruffled. And as she went to knock again, Maria knelt down at the door and flipped up the letterbox to speak through it.

'Miss Page, please . . . may we come in? I live on the square too . . .' Maria began . . . at number seven,' she paused. Still there was no response. Oh what the heck, she thought. They hadn't got anywhere so far by being sensitive.

'We know about the secret tunnels . . . under the garden. Is that how Mina escaped?' Maria continued.

LT's jaw hit the pavement. She couldn't believe Maria had said it. But she'd said it all right. A million and one things ran through LT's mind in that moment. What if they were wrong? What if this woman wasn't even the housekeeper? Even if she was Miss Page, what if she knew nothing about the King family? They'd just shared the biggest piece of their puzzle with a complete stranger. But before she could say a word to Maria, the door opened.

Bless, Maria, she thought. *Oh to be young and reckless again.*

Smoothing over her frizzy grey hair, the lady stood expressionless in the hallway.

'Perhaps you'd better come in,' she said quietly, closing the door behind them. 'But only until I ask you to leave,' she added.

'Of course,' LT said. 'Thank you.'

Maria felt a wave of relief and excitement. And keeping her left thumb pressed down firmly on the receiver button on the walkie-talkie watch in her pocket, she followed the occupant of forty-five Beaufort Square into her living room.

'They're in!' Molly squealed to the girls as she grabbed the walkie-talkie watch from the table.

'No way!' Danya and Honey said together.

'Listen! She's using the radio so we can hear. Quick!' she cried, as the others gathered round.

'I'd offer you some tea or coffee but I don't drink either, so there is none,' the old lady said as she sat down. 'Please have a seat.'

'Thank you so much for seeing us – Miss Page, is it?' LT said, keen to check they had Charles King's housekeeper in front of them.

The old lady nodded.

'We'll be as brief as we possibly can so as not to take up too much of your valuable time. As I said at the door, I'm Luscious Tangerella, editor of the *Gazette* and this is my . . . my colleague, Maria Fitzfoster.'

Colleague . . . Maria blushed.

'As Maria mentioned, she and her family reside at number seven Beaufort Square, and have recently discovered an underground network of tunnels and a central shelter located underneath the residents' garden. We wondered, as someone who has lived here for a while, whether perhaps you might be able to tell us a little of their history?' LT continued.

Maria thought how amazing it was that Miss Page hadn't even flinched when they mentioned the tunnels or the bomb shelter. She clearly knew of their existence.

'How long have you lived here, Miss Page?' Maria asked.

'I moved here in 1958 to care for the previous owner of the house.'

'Mr King?' Maria asked. She couldn't help herself.

'Yes,' Miss Page said simply.

'And you've been here ever since?' Maria said.

'Yes,' she said again.

'And were you aware of the underground shelter below the square?'

Maria was clearly on a roll and LT wasn't about to stop her.

'I was aware, yes.' Miss Page answered. 'Mr King told me everything I needed to know before he died. He left the house and everything in it to me, you know, so it would make sense that he should inform me of any secret tunnels that might come with it.'

'I see,' LT said. 'That was a lovely gesture. He had no other surviving next of kin to speak of?'

Nice one, LT, Maria and the girls thought.

'The King family history is a complicated one and perhaps one best left unspoken,' Miss Page said thoughtfully.

She had to be in her eighties herself, thought Maria. She had such sadness in her eyes. Such gloom. And was it any wonder? It was freezing in that house. There can't ever have been any central heating installed.

Miss Page saw Maria shiver and her eyes softened. 'I'm sorry, dear. Are you cold? With it just being me here, I tend to light the fire to warm the place up. I never bother with radiators.'

'I'm fine – thank you,' Maria said, and then everything came tumbling out just like it had in LT's office. Once she started talking, she found she couldn't stop.

She told Miss Page all about shadowing LT and the truth about how she and her friends at number forty-four had stumbled across the tunnels quite by accident. She told of their excitement at finding such an adventure on their own doorstep. How their love of the garden led on to the fountain and the beautiful mysterious ballerina, and how they'd decided to investigate who she was, learning that Mr King had lived at number forty-five with his only daughter, who had disappeared.

Miss Page sat in complete silence throughout. LT watched Maria with pride. The innocent way she delivered her information was captivating. If this couldn't get the old lady to talk, nothing would.

'Did you ever know Mina King, Miss Page? Charles's daughter who went missing at the start of the war.'

Miss Page sat up suddenly.

'No, I told you, I came long after the disappearance of Miss King. The loss of Mina broke Mr King's heart. When I arrived he was fatally wounded by grief. I nursed him and cared for him the best I could until he died and left me here in this big old house, all alone, with only memories for company.'

'But . . .' Maria started. 'Did he . . . Mr King ever talk to you about what really happened to his daughter? We know she ran away . . .'

But she was stopped short.

'Please leave. I have nothing more to say to you. I have already shared more than Mr King would have liked,' Miss Page said, tears in her eyes.

'But . . .' Maria said.

'You promised you would go when I asked,' Miss Page said, hobbling to the front door, which she held open.

'Thank you for your time, Miss Page,' LT said. 'We are sorry to have bothered you.'

'It's so frustrating!' Maria groaned when she was putting the final touches to their hats with the rest of the girls. 'She one-hundred-per-cent knew more than she told us. I feel like going back over there now and demanding the truth.'

'Mimi, don't. We've been lucky to get this far. Poor Miss Page is eighty if she's a day and goodness knows what could happen if you stress her out again. Let LT deal with it now. The article will be superb! You know it will,' Molly said, giving her sister a hug.

'Hear! Hear!' Danya said, pretending to toast Maria with her lemonade.

'To Mina Ballerina. May she rest in peace . . . wherever she is,' Maria said.

To Mina Ballerina!' the girls cried, clinking their glasses until there was more lemonade on their hats than in their tummies.

15

A Summer Party to Remember

'Everyone say summer breeeeeze,' Brian Fitzfoster said as everyone in the household gathered together for the usual garden party family photo.

'SUMMER BREEEEEEZE!' they cried.

'Super!' Brian said, as he scanned back through the photos he'd taken.

'You jump in, Mr F,' said Sally suddenly. 'It wouldn't be a Fitzfoster family photo without all of the Fitzfosters in it!'

'Why how thoughtful, Sally. I don't mind if I do,' he said and slipped into the middle beside his wife.

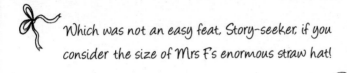

Which was not an easy feat, Story-seeker, if you consider the size of Mrs F's enormous straw hat!

As Sally snapped away, she thought again how lucky she was to be part of such a lovely family. She looked over at her own mum, who stood chattering away to Mrs Dundas. Maggie Sudbury had, of course, been invited up from Wilton house to spend the party weekend with her daughter and the family, and was absolutely loving being with them all again.

'Sally, darling, if you've got your shot, I think perhaps Mrs Dundas and I had better bring up the fruit punch! Guests will start arriving at any moment,' Maggie said, immediately scurrying off to the kitchen.

'Don't we all look divine!' Molly said, admiring their handiwork.

You could have filled a dozen plump pillows with the number of pink feathers she'd stuck to her hat. Maria, on the other hand, was sporting quite an understated boater with roses; Pippa's was a very stylish French beret with a smattering of flowers, feathers and glitter. But the quirkiest of all was Sally with her massive bird's-nest hat which she'd woven herself using twigs from the garden, filled with half a dozen real eggs (hard-boiled in case any fell off) and a pretend bird on the top.

Put it this way, Story-seeker: you'd have found it tricky to keep a straight face if you'd been there.

'Cover me!' Maria announced suddenly, noticing her mum frantically searching on the other side of the room, then making a beeline for her. It was too late. There was nowhere to hide.

'Maria, I wonder, would you mind hopping on the hall piano for an hour, just while people arrive? It totally slipped my mind to book someone!'

'Oh but Mu-um!' Maria said and then stopped. It suddenly dawned on her that the absence of a piano player might just be the one thing that tipped her mum over the edge.

'Sure I will,' she said. 'But only if Pippa sings!'

'Ooooh, how marvellous. Would you, Pippa?' Linda said.

'And to hear me?' Maria joked.

Pippa did what anyone with zero choice in the matter would do. She smiled and said, 'It would be my pleasure, Mrs F!'

Linda thanked the girls, but not before putting

Sally and Molly on coat duty, and waltzed off into the living room to check nothing else had gone wrong.

'Thanks for that, Maria!' Pippa scowled.

'Oh, come on. You're not telling me you're not desperate to give us a song, are you? Come Missy – sing your little heart out. Never know who might walk through that door and hear you!' Maria grinned, at which point the front door bell went.

The two girls raced over to the piano and began to play.

'See!' Maria said suddenly, as Pippa turned around to see the first guests arrive in the form of Mr Fuller, her music mentor and Mrs Fuller, his wife and the girls' favourite teacher.

'Sing, girlfriend!' Maria said with a giggle.

As the never-ending trail of lavishly adorned guests continued to arrive, Molly was starting to get a little bit jumpy about the fact that Danya and Honey hadn't got there yet.

'I thought they'd be the first ones through the front door. Can't wait to see what they've done with their hats. Honey texted me to say they'd had a last-minute brainwave and that they were brilliant,' Molly said, hanging up her fiftieth coat of the evening.

'They'll be along soon. Weren't their parents supposed to be home from Norfolk this afternoon? Maybe they've been held up,' Sally whispered.

'Gosh – do you think Mrs Sawyer will have a baby bump yet? I love babies,' Molly said.

'Not sure, but either way I think we've managed to talk Danya and Honey round on that subject. I actually think they're excited about having a baby brother or sister to cuddle now,' Pippa said.

Ding, dong . . .

'Oh, hello, your ears must have been burning!' Molly said as she opened the door to their best friends.

'Hello!' Danya and Honey said and as they stood next to each other, the huge flower-covered letters on their hats spelled out PAR–TY.

'Brilliant!' Molly said, not entirely convinced. Their hats only made sense when their heads were together – otherwise it just looked like Danya had random 'PAR' letters on her head and Honey 'TY'.

'Mum, Dad, you remember the girls . . . Molly and Sally from the Fitzfosters' party in Sussex,' Danya said, re-introducing her parents.

'Indeed I do. What a home you have there on the

coast with its very own smugglers' hideout below. I didn't stop talking about it for weeks. Most intriguing,' Mr Sawyer said, handing Molly his coat.

'Oh, thanks, we all love it down there too! And congratulations on the baby, by the way. We think it's just magical,' Molly said, talking to Mrs Sawyer, who blushed.

'Why, thank you, ladies. It is rather exciting, isn't it? My girls will just have to teach him or her everything they know if this bump is to be half as wonderful as they are,' Mrs Sawyer answered.

Danya and Honey were grinning from ear to ear.

'Graham and Tina, how wonderful to see you both. How are your poor parents and their house? I couldn't think of anything worse!' Linda Fitzfoster said as she came into the hall and spotted the Sawyers.

'They're on the mend but honestly, I've never seen such a mess!' Tina Sawyer said.

'And the twins have told me your news. How fabulous! You know where we are if you ever need a sitter for the night when the time comes!' Linda Fitzfoster said, smiling.

And then, turning to Danya and Honey, she said, 'Girls, you know your way around; won't you show your parents into the reception room and get them a drink? I'll just finish up here.'

'Sure,' Danya and Honey cried and led their parents away.

'Maria, Pippa . . .' she called. 'You've been complete superstars but do take a break now. You've been going for a whole hour and we're so grateful. What a wonderful welcome you've given everyone.'

Maria and Pippa had been rather enjoying themselves, especially when they saw poor Sally and Molly being run ragged between door and cloakroom duty.

'Maria, Molly, here's the guest list. Try your best through the scribbles . . . the printer decided to go on strike before I could print a final copy but everyone's name should be here. Molly, you'll remember who's here already. Tick them off and see who's missing. Don't want us all disappearing off into the garden for the hat winner announcement until everyone's here.'

'No problem, mum,' Maria said, casting her eye down the list and already starting to tick off names.

'Mum, don't forget to tell Dad to have a good look at everyone's hats this year before he makes a decision about who first prize is going to. Remember last year he totally forgot so just picked the biggest, loudest and nearest hat to him, which defeats the object of us all having gone to so much trouble . . . I mean, where's the incentive in that?' Molly said, never more serious in her life.

Linda Fitzfoster burst into giggles, which was a relief to everyone.

'Molly, darling, there really is no one else like you, which, given that you are a twin, is a complete miracle. I have news for you, though. It isn't Dad who's doing the judging this year.'

'It isn't?' Molly and Maria asked.

'No. Actually there's someone here far better qualified to take that decision. I'll leave it to your deductive powers and the guest list to work out who tonight's judge is. I don't think you'll be disappointed,' and with that, she marched back to the party.

'Have you worked out who the judge is yet?' Molly said. 'Honey and I have put our thinking caps on . . . ha! Get it? Thinking caps for a hat competition! Ha! and we're convinced it's a designer.'

'Well, the only two names left here I can't identify are Lauren McIntosh and Philip Treacy – both of them are—'

'Give me that!' Molly said, snatching the board.

'Philip Treacy . . . *the* Philip Treacy?' she said, spotting his name.

The girls looked blankly back at her.

'Grrrrr! Come on! Surely you've heard of him? He's only the most famous hat designer of all time! Oh my days, I think I might faint. How did I miss him come through that door?' Molly said, fanning her face with her hand. 'Oh, girls. What a competition this is going to be. I hope I win . . . sorry . . . but I do!' Molly said, her eye now firmly on the prize, which of course had nothing to do with the practically human-sized box of chocolates, but the satisfaction of having the Philip Treacy thinking she was the best.

'Can anyone read this last name?' Pippa asked. 'I think your mum may have scribbled it in a bit of a hurry. It looks like *Leeepage*.'

'No idea,' Molly said.

'Gosh, not even I can make sense of that and usually I'm so good at deciphering our parents' spider-scrawl!' Maria said.

Suddenly Danya put her hand up to her brow. 'Oh, I completely forgot to tell you guys. You sort of invited Miss Page . . . see, Leeeepage is Lizzie Page.'

'What?' Pippa, Sally, Molly, Honey and Maria all exploded at once.

'Look, don't worry about it. There's no way she'll come – it was quite by accident, when I was asking Postman Peter for the name of who lived at number forty-five . . .' and Danya went on to tell the whole story of how he took the invitation from her and posted it himself. 'I thought I'd best mention it to your mum, just in case. She won't come. You said yourself, Maria, you don't think she's left the house for years.'

The girls were silent. No one really knew what to say or think.

'Come on, let's go and get something to drink. I'm parched!' Pippa said.

'Yes let's,' Honey said. 'Molly and I need to do some serious Philip Treacy stalking!'

Ding dong . . .

Maria, her hand already gripping the latch, opened the door once more and there, pretty much at the same eye-level, her previously wild grey hair swept tidily into a bun at the side under a beautiful dusky pink velvet bonnet, stood the occupant of number forty-five Beaufort Square.

16

The Truth, the Whole Truth, and Nothing but the Truth

The six girls stood in stunned silence in the Fitzfosters' hallway. Maria took a deep breath.

'Good evening, Maria,' Miss Page said, sensing her attendance might have come as a bit of a shock.

'Good evening,' Maria stammered. 'Welcome, Miss Page. We're so delighted you could make it.'

'Thank you so much for the kind invitation. Had it not been for you ladies popping over this morning, I might never have started tackling the post – something I loathe and deliberately only do once a month. I might have missed it altogether. It's many, many years since I received an invitation to anything so I thought, why not?'

'Well I'm so pleased you did. May we take your coat?' Maria held out her hand as she welcomed their guest.

Molly moved quickly to retrieve it.

'Oh, this is my twin sister, Molly,' Maria said. 'And these are our friends Pippa and Sally, and Danya and Honey, who are also twins . . . and your neighbours, in fact. They live at number forty-four,' Maria continued.

'How wonderful,' Miss Page said, shaking hands with all of them and trying to make a mental note of their names.

'Would you like to come this way to join the main party?' Molly said.

'Oh not just yet, thank you. Maria and I have some unfinished business to attend to . . .' She paused to look at Maria, whose eyes blazed with excitement. 'Only if it's a good time?' Miss Page continued.

'Really? I mean, thank you! I mean, great! Yes please,' Maria stammered again.

Molly came to the rescue. 'Maria, why don't you take Miss Page into the study where it's quiet.'

'Good idea, Moll,' Maria said gratefully.

Then turning to Miss Page she said, 'Would you mind if all the girls came with me to hear what you have to say? It's just we've all worked so hard and wondered so much about what might have happened here in the square, it doesn't seem right for us all not to share this moment.'

'Why, of course. And perhaps you should bring a pen and paper with you, Maria. We wouldn't want Miss Tangerella to miss a single detail, now would we?' Miss Page said, with a grin. 'Oh and girls, please call me Lizzie. It makes me feel young again.'

Maria could have kissed her. This was it! Her big break! Not only was Lizzie Page about to tell her everything she knew about Mina Ballerina, but she was actually giving her permission to publish the story.

They made themselves comfortable, with Sally, the last through the door, having dashed for a tray of lemonade for the girls and a glass of pink champagne for Lizzie.

'Oh, how thoughtful. I haven't had champagne for so long,' she said, savouring the first sip as it fizzed deliciously in her mouth.

'Please understand, girls, I can only tell you what I know. There will most likely be huge chunks that are missing and probably even bigger chunks of time that I have forgotten. Now, are you sitting comfortably?'

They nodded as if in deep hypnosis.

'Charles and Olga King lived in Moscow until Olga

sadly died when their only daughter, Wilhelmina, was five. Charles was so heartbroken, he couldn't bear to stay there, so decided to move to London, to Beaufort Square. Mina was an excellent student but her real talent lay in ballet, which she inherited from her mother, who was a dancer at the Bolshoi Ballet in Moscow. Naturally her father did everything in his power to nurture her talent to the highest level, so that one day his daughter might achieve her dream of becoming a world-famous ballerina. Something of which her mother would have been immensely proud. He even built her her very own dance studio in the cellar at number forty-five so that she could practise around the clock . . .'

The girls shot each other knowing glances.

'Mina gained such recognition for her talents that she was contacted by Sadler's Wells, to audition to star in the first national ballet tour of its kind. This was it: her dream was about to become a reality, but on the eve of the first show, Charles panicked. He suddenly told his daughter that she could not dance and they had a terrible argument. It ended with Mina running away, even though it meant her giving up everything she loved, ballet and her father, and him losing his most precious possession – his daughter.'

'So she definitely wasn't kidnapped?' Molly said, wanting that confirmed, once and for all.

'Not at all,' Lizzie continued. 'That night, shortly before midnight, Mina left their home using the underground tunnels, exiting at the church and turning her back on everything she had ever known or loved. She was angry with her father for destroying her dreams and for refusing to explain why to her. She made up her mind never to come back. No one would find her. It would be as though she had vanished . . .'

'Oh my goodness!' Honey said, so ensconced in the story she couldn't help herself.

'So angry and adamant that her father should never find her, she decided it would be better to keep moving and fell into a life on the road when she joined a circus as a magician's assistant. As the years went on, Mina finally found happiness marrying a trapeze artist, but this happiness was short-lived when, five years later, her poor husband died, leaving her alone. It was only then that she thought she would try returning to her father. When she arrived back in Beaufort Square, she didn't even know if he was still alive . . .'

'And did she see him . . . her father . . . tell me she saw him before he died . . .' Molly begged, tearfully.

'Oh, I can't bear it,' Sally sniffed. 'This is the saddest

story I've ever heard.' Lizzie reached out and held Molly's and Sally's hands. 'Oh, girls. Please don't be upset. I'm happy to say she did see him. Mina and Charles were reunited and lived together there for a few years until he died. In fact, when Charles King opened the door to his only daughter, he was already sick, but I think seeing her again breathed life back into his bones and he lived for as long as he could to spend time with her,' Lizzie said, smiling. Her eyes were no longer dull and grey, but dancing in the candlelight.

'Oh, I'm so happy!' Molly sighed.

'Yes,' Honey said. 'Thank goodness they had some time together to put right the wrongs.'

'It's just so sad Mina never got to realise her dancing dream,' Pippa said.

The girls continued to chat, absorbing all the answers they'd just been given by the wonderful Lizzie Page. Lizzie watched, basking in the glow of their youth.

'So you knew her!' Maria exclaimed suddenly, remembering. 'You said you didn't know Mina. But you must have . . . your paths must have crossed at number forty-five.'

Lizzie put her champagne glass down on the table.

'No, Maria,' she started to say. 'You are mistaken. I never knew—'

'Yes, I know what you said. But you must have. You said Mina came home to spend the last few years with her father, but you also said you nursed him until he died. There must have been a time when you were both there.'

Maria paused. She was onto something . . . Lizzie was lying about something, she could feel it. What was it?!

Lizzie was silent, her eyes once again a dull grey.

'You said it was you who looked after him when he had no one else, which is why, when he died, he left the house to you . . . left everything to you. Why, why would he do that, if he knew Mina was alive? If Mina was at the house, living with him, caring for hi—' Maria stopped. Her hand flew to her mouth as she gasped.

Then Danya gasped, followed by Pippa and then Sally. Honey and Molly looked more confused than ever.

Maria stood up, then knelt on the floor in front of Lizzie. Taking her hand she said, 'It's OK. Oh my stars, it's finally OK. We know. We know it's you . . . Mina!'

Honey and Molly caught on and gasped, hands flying to their mouths.

'It's always been you, hiding behind Lizzie Page, but it's OK now. You can trust us,' Maria said.

A single tear rolled down Lizzie Page's face, followed by another and another and suddenly she smiled. The relief was overwhelming. Finally, someone had called her by her name.

'And Lizzie, from Elizabeth, your middle name,' Danya said.

'It's true,' she said. I am Wilhelmina Elizabeth King. Page was my married name. I decided I would keep using it so as not to attract any attention after my father's death, but actually it's all such a long time ago – the world has changed – and I feel differently now.'

'It's so wonderful to finally meet you, Mina,' Pippa said, offering Mina a tissue.

'We've been searching for you for ever such a long time,' Molly said.

'I can't tell you what a relief it is to tell someone . . . to tell all of you,' Mina said. 'Until you knocked on my door today, I thought the past should remain in the past, but I was wrong. After you left, I finally realised I had nothing to fear by telling the truth. I've watched you girls picnicking by the statue my father had erected in my memory. Never in a million years did I imagine that you were wondering about who or where I was,' Mina said, wiping her eyes.

'Thank you, girls, for releasing me from my cage. I feel like a genie who's been freed from the lamp. Finally I can hold my head high and stop pretending that Mina King doesn't exist.'

'Well, Miss King . . . how would you feel about being re-introduced into society and meeting our parents? I know they'll be over the moon to finally meet you too,' Molly said.

'It would be my pleasure,' Mina said. 'But do you think I could have another glass of champagne? I did so enjoy the first.'

The girls laughed and escorted their new friend out of the study.

Maria knelt on the rug in complete silence. Had what just happened, really just happened? Had Mina really been there the whole time? Quickly she checked her watch . . . hopefully the *Gazette* hadn't gone to print yet. LT was going to have to make some last-minute changes!'

17

Eyes on the Prize

'Well, my goodness gracious me,' Linda Fitzfoster said in amazement. 'I can't quite believe it. And all this time, Miss King, you've been just over the road. What an enormous pleasure it is to finally meet you.'

'Isn't it incredible, Mum?' Molly said, wondering where Maria had disappeared off to.

'My dear lady, you have had our girls in a complete spin trying to solve your mystery, and I am so proud of them. We couldn't have hoped for a more wonderful outcome,' said Brian Fitzfoster.

'Mr and Mrs Fitzfoster, your girls and their friends are a credit to you. I feel as though my life can finally begin again, thanks to their dogged determination. Thank you for having me this evening,' Mina said, raising her glass.

'Actually, Miss King, there is someone here who I'd love you to meet,' Linda said, scanning the room. 'Ah yes, there she is. Won't you come with me?'

Seeing Mrs Dundas and Maggie usher the last of the guests through the residents' garden gate, Brian Fitzfoster stood in front of Mina's fountain and tapped on his champagne glass to get everyone's attention.

Ting, ting, ting.

Molly and Honey tore their glances away from Philip Treacy for the first time in about twenty minutes.

'Ladies and gentlemen, thank you all so much for coming to our annual summer party. The time has now come to announce the winner of this year's competition – and sadly there can be only one winner. And judging this year, we have the King of Millinery, Mr Philip Treacy,' Brian Fitzfoster said, commencing a round of applause.

'Thank you, Brian. I'm not one for speeches so I'll be brief. There are so many entries this evening from which I'll be drawing inspiration for my next collection, but there is one which stands out from the rest. The winner has an eye for balance and cutting-edge design, and I'd be only too happy for her to assist me at some point in her fashion career, should she so desire. Ladies and gentlemen, I give you your winner this evening, Miss Molly Fitzfoster!'

It was a *Prince Charming* moment. Molly heard her name called, but then everything seemed to turn to ringing in her ears. She was frozen to the spot until Honey gave her an almighty shove in the right direction.

'Moll! You did it! You did it!'

'Go Molly!'

Everyone clapped and cheered as Molly went to shake Philip Treacy's hand.

'Truly magnificent,' he said. 'Well done, Molly. And I meant what I said, should you ever need an introduction to the fashion industry!'

'Oh thank you, thank you!' Molly said, blushing so much she clashed with her pink feathers.

Now this was a perfect ending, she thought to herself as she had her photo taken with the huge box of chocolates. She couldn't wait to tuck into that with the rest of the girls when they were back at their beloved L'Etoile.

What a fabulous night!

18

Goodbye London, Hello L'Etoile

'Mina looked about twenty years younger this morning when I bumped into her on the steps. She was even watering some hanging baskets she's planted since the party,' Danya said as the girls lay down on their picnic blanket, gazing up at the fountain.

'Did you speak to her? How is she?' Maria asked. 'Did she say anything about yesterday's article? I thought LT captured it all brilliantly!'

'She said she'd seen it and that she couldn't believe it had all happened to her. She said reading her story in black and white like that, it felt like it had happened to someone else,' Honey said.

'It can only be a good thing. It means she's finally moving on,' Pippa said, feeling proud to have played a part in that.

'Did you know Sadlers' Wells have decided to honour her with a lifetime achievement award after the final performance of Swan Lake on Friday? She'll have to go onto the stage to receive it and everything,' Maria said.

'No way! Amazing!' everyone answered.

'LT gave them a heads up on the story and they were desperate to do something for her,' Maria continued.

'Ooooh! Can we go? I'd love to be there,' Molly said.

'Definitely! We're all going!'

'What a brilliant way to end the holidays. It's been eventful as always,' Pippa said.

'Let's just hope next term brings us something fun to get our teeth into.' Danya said.

'Well if we've learned anything this week, it's that the answer to the biggest of mysteries can sometimes be right under our noses, so I think we all need to be extra vigilant when we go back,' Maria said.

'She's right,' Sally said. 'We'll have to not sit back and wait for the action to find us this time. It's up to us to find the action!'

'You said it, Agent Sudbury!' Molly giggled and then turned to Honey. 'Now, let's get our _www.looklikeastar. com_ order in for the new term . . . don't want to turn up dressed in last season's fashions, do we?'

'For heaven's sake!' Maria said, rolling her eyes at Danya. 'Are you sure those two weren't switched at birth? Molly so should have been a Sawyer!'

'Tell me about it!' Danya said. 'Perhaps we should swap!'

But of course, the twins wouldn't have swapped in a million years, Story-seeker. It just meant they'd have to make it their mission to spend even more time together. That way, they'd never miss each other, or an adventure!

A Guide to Molly Fitzfoster's Favourite Sayings

CO = Chill Out

WAYL = What Are You Like?

TDF = To Die For

AYKM = Are You Kidding Me?

WATC = What Are The Chances?

OCYA = Of Course You Are

BTW = By The Way

INLID = I'll Never Live It Down

*Join the girls for more fabulous fun-filled
adventures in the School for Stars series . . .*

First Term at L'Etoile

On the first day of term at L'Etoile, School for Stars,
twins Maria and Molly Fitzfoster meet
Pippa Burrows who's won a song-writing
scholarship to the school. The talented trio share
the same dreams of super-stardom and become best
friends. But will their friendship stand up against
Lucifette Marciano's plans to wreck their chances
and claim fame for herself?

978 1 4440 0811 1

£4.99

Second Term at L'Etoile

The Christmas holidays are over and best friends Molly, Maria and Pippa return to their beloved L'Etoile, School for Stars for more fun and adventure. A midnight hunt for lost treasure, a playful puppy with a twinkle in her eye and a royal visit are just some of the things they're about to share. They may be friends forever, but will they make it to the end of term without getting expelled?

978 1 4440 0813 5

£4.99

Third Term at L'Etoile

Our favourite friends forever are back for another exciting term. A television show comes to school and plans are afoot for a glittering end of term charity fundraiser. But as you know, Story-seeker, there's never an adventure without a drama at L'Etoile, and with Molly's Hollywood audition, the dreaded summer exams and the return of Lucifette Marciano with her truly hideous friend, we're just not sure how the girls are going to survive . . .

978 1 4440 0815 9

£4.99

Summer Holiday Mystery

Molly and Maria fly home from Hollywood
for a rest, but their summer holiday by the sea
with Pippa and Sally is anything but relaxing!
Strange howling noises in the night, a disappearing
puppy, a secret cave and kidnap lead the four
BFFs on a hair-raising adventure. But will they
solve the mystery in time to save the day?

978 1 4440 0817 3

£4.99

Double Trouble at L'Etoile

Molly, Maria, Pippa and Sally are all set for their
second year at L'Etoile, School for Stars. After the
excitement of their first year and holiday adventures
they've promised their parents an event-free term.
But we all know that's not going to happen, don't
we? A new pair of twins in school and some ghostly
goings-on mean the BFFs have to get their skates on
to solve a spooky mystery.

978 1 4440 1455 6

£5.99

the orion star

★ ★ ★

CALLING ALL GROWN-UPS!
Sign up for **the orion star** newsletter to
hear about your favourite authors and exclusive
competitions, plus details of how children
can join our 'Story Stars' review panel.

Sign up at:

www.orionbooks.co.uk/orionstar

Follow us 🐦 @the_orionstar
Find us 📘 facebook.com/TheOrionStar